The Wisdom of Beasts and Cavemen

Short Stories
Written in Rhyme

by

Allen (Pud) Deters

v25-1013

Table of Contents

SAMMI'S LAND BRIDGE

When the Ice Age was bad as could
    be
And ocean levels were falling,
A walkway rose up in the Bearing
    Sea.
A brave new world was calling!

Young Sammi and her Stone Age
    pals
Discovered this road to the east
And as typical boys and gals
They meant to explore it at least.

But the village boss, the shaman,
Quickly stopped the young fools,
A reaction all too common
With bosses who make the rules.

"Woe!" said he. "This has ruined the
    sea!
Bring shovels. Dig a channel through
    it.
This land bridge was never meant to
    be.
Demolish it! Just do it."

He left the details to his staffers,
A bean counter and a clerk.
They were also fat old gaffers
Who couldn't do spadework.

The villagers obeyed the boss
And breached the Ice Age causeway.
And late that night water trickled
    across
After a long, sweaty day.

It was quite a feat with Stone Age
    tools
To tackle climate change disorder.
Admit it, you thought they were
    fools,
But they restored the continental
    border!

By dawn the trickle dried up, went
    away.
Sea levels had dropped below.
They would have to dig every day!
"This is stupid", said Sammi. "Let's
    go".

She headed to Alaska with friends
And all the commonfolk followed
    her.
To a happy ending? That depends.
But they smelled freedom, for sure!

ROMANCE, AMERICAN STYLE

A New World offered new ambitions
So the girls did what they had to do
About junking some Old-World
    traditions
When they moved on to the New.

Like the popular 'Head-Bashing'.
Guys claimed wives with a club, a
    bludgeon,
And it wasn't very dashing
To be kayoed by some old
    curmudgeon.

To address this, some girls in the
    lead
Held up the entire tribe
They were not-yet-bashed and saw a
    need
For a Shaman they could bribe.

Greedy fellows vied for the role.
Men voted. Who would they elect?
Money changed hands, ballots were
    stole.

The greediest guy won. That's
    perfect!

He invited the girls and ladies
To a prayer session he'd been
    dreading.
But they didn't give him Hades.
They prayed for expensive weddings!

Weddings? He checked his price list.
They were very high. Bashings were
    free.
He could be rich! But they did insist
The clubs must go. That's how it
    must be.

All this the Shaman decreed
And wedding costs have since been
    dreaded.
But girls had a right to be freed!
Except now thcy want to be wedded.

TO BE OR NOT TO BE

Eventually the Ice Age ended.
The lands awoke, no longer frozen.
So Great Spirit, as intended,
Introduced Biblical Men, His
    Chosen.

That news spread around the Earth
And all who were offended
Were offered tryouts to prove their
    worth,
Which lots of hominids attended:

Roving tribes, apes and
    Neanderthals,
Cro-Magnans and chimpanzees,
Sasquatch and other oddballs,
Plus monkeys who swung down from
    the trees.

All expected to move up in class
But the Lord, Almighty talent scout,
Brought a red pencil because – alas!
Most of the hopefuls would flunk out.

First off, tails were a disqualifier
For humanity, what can I say?
So the monkees were asked to retire.
It just wasn't their day.

The chimp and gorilla bands
Had calloused knuckles on their
    hands
They spoke mostly in beastly roars
And walked like animals on all fours.

They did have opposable thumbs
So they could learn to draw, which
    was nice.
And possibly count and do sums.
But mostly they just picked lice.

Their audition drew hilarity
And Great Spirit waved them away.
His ruling was meant for posterity -
But that could be changing today!

Now we wallow in an equity bog
With – ugh! – animals. That's the
    new rule.
If a student says they're a cat or dog
They get a litter box at school.

It's coming. There'll be class-action
    suits
On behalf of chimpanzees
To make schools accept the hairy
    brutes
And some court will entertain their
    pleas.

What about Great Spirit's precedent?
Can our courts vacate *that,* on a
    whim?
You bet, and they won't be hesitant.
Our Supreme Court will overrule
    HIM.

Laws are laws, even if hairbrained.
So prepare for random poopers.
The chimps will not be potty-trained

So your school will need pooper-
    scoopers.

ℴℴ

Meanwhile, a few thousand years
    prior,
Some auditioners had found success.
All the cave-people could make fire
And had language, more or less.

That showed some humanity
But did they have worthwhile souls?
Great Spirit disliked profanity.
It reminded Him of the trolls.

Bad posture would flunk for probable
    cause.
Humans are meant to stand straight.
Cave dwellers did, which was good,
    because
Slouching was a goblin trait.

Seeking further sign of human touch
A little closer to His heart,
Cultured, but not sissified as such,
He took notice of their art.

They wore jewelry, that long ago,
In good taste, not just clutteral,
And most could sing quite well,
    although
Neanderthals were gutteral.

Lastly they all drew Ice Age
    mammals
Painting them on the cave walls.
Most drew mammoths, wolves or
    camels.
Cro-Magnans drew Neanderthals.

So both evolution and creation
Had their troubles right away.
And maybe we're here on probation
Because it's no different today.

FLAT EARTH THEORY

It's been hard, being a Flat-Earther
With doubters like Pythagoras.
Then other scholars pushed the
    doubt further.
But all of them were superfluous.

Pythagoras knew his triangles.
His proofs were unblinking.
But a flat earth has no angles!
So he was guilty of over-thinking.

That's fun, debunking a Great
    Scholar!
Back then, Flat-Earthers were many.
Round earthers could hoot and
    holler,
But where's the proof? They didn't
    have any.

Yee-ha! Flat-Earthers were right
For thousands of years, and more.
It was the heyday of the not-so-
    bright!
Then ship captains began to explore.

They sailed West and came to the
    East

Which inferred that the earth was
    round.
The ranks of Flat-Earthers
    decreased.
The rest of us went underground.

The round earth news made us weary
But we still thought it was bull.
We stuck to our old theory
Because the oceans stayed full.

We consulted mystics, magicians,
Searched libraries for advice.
Then came word from the
    expeditions.
Everything at the bottom was ice.

We were wiped out by the truth!
Ice was reported by every ship.
It explained the full oceans, forsooth:
The ice would prevent any drip.

Flat-Earthers disbanded that day.
And disavowed our positions.
We walked it all back, all the way.
Now we're successful politicians.

ORIGIN OF FIRE

Way back in Ice Age history
Fire was worshipped and cherished.
How to make it was still a mystery
But you either had it, or you
    perished.

That's where the Servants came in,
To guard the sacred fire with their
    lives.
The job was passed to their next-of-
    kin
And it came with seven wives.

Well? Someone had to do the chores.
A communal fire was built each day
To roast the beast and dry wet
    drawers.
Each night the hot coals were locked
    away.

Behind that the Servant ran a racket.
Daily offerings were expected.
He thought up the "Tax Bracket",
And lots of taxes were collected.

One day some kids created a
    sensation
By sparking fire using rocks.
It caused a balloon of elation
But the Servant popped it, the old
    fox.

He alleged there'd been a break-in

To the forbidden Fire Pot,
That sacred coals had been taken
And these kids were behind the plot.

The honored Servant was believed.
He had stature, the old swine.
The kids were dismissed and peeved.
The Servant celebrated with wine.

That night he awoke, quite besotted.
Had bladder pressure. He knew he
    would.
He found the chamber pot. He
    squatted.
He let fly. Ooh, that felt good!

Let's call it his last official act,
Because it would doom the old liar.
He had used the wrong pot. In fact,
He had drowned the sacred fire!

They kicked him out into the wild
To fetch new fire in his soiled pot.
All seven wives laughed and smiled.
No one cared if he came back or not.

The kids showed off their fire-
    making.
For free, when they could've been
    sellers.
They were naïve about profit-taking.
That must wait for the Rockefellers.

THE GYPSY MOTH

Pity the wandering pilgrim
Perhaps with no home of their own
Afoot, forlorn, their future so dim
So down on their luck, all alone.

You pass as they hold out their
    thumb
But their plight is too much to abide.
Oh, sure. They might be a bum
But your heart melts. You offer a
    ride.

That is the Gypsy Moth ploy
So the flightless girl can lay eggs
In a brand new forest – oh joy!
And she'll get her ride if she begs.

A monarch once heard that lie
When the temperature was near zero:
"Just a short ride, please, then
    goodbye",
The gypsy begged her would-be
    hero.

So the monarch carried the bum.
She was fat. Her belly was huge.
That was eggs, but of that she was
    mum,

To keep secret the subterfuge.

When the monarch had to rest
The moth snapped off a shard of ice
And would have plunged it into her
    breast
Unless she flew on. No more nice.

A nighthawk eyed them suspiciously
In a muderous mood,
And circled inauspiciously
Being no friend of the gypsy brood.

A river appeared. On the far shore
Loomed living trees, a tall stand.
It was all a gypsy could ask for.
Hallelujah! The Promised Land!

She meant to kill the butterfly.
Just for secrecy. No one's fault.
But the monarch said "Goodbye",
And did a somersault.

As she fell toward the rushing water
The bum saw two fates. Would she
    drown?
Or just be hawk food for slaughter?
But a big fish gulped her down.

THE CAST IRON POT

It was first known in China B.C.
Where it changed local eating habits.
It cooked rice and veggies quite
    savory
And also wild game, like rabbits.

A big pot full would feed a village
But good cheer often turned to
    screaming.
Alas, dragons would feast and pillage
When they smelled the juicy meat
    steaming.

When the brutes licked out the pot
The slobber burned into the metal
Which was then auctioned off for
    near naught
Because of the stink in the kettle.

It still looked useful, although buyers
    –
Mongols, Russians, even the French,
Sterilized it over their fires
It retained the dragon stench.

A Norwegian lad used it for fish,
To soak them in poisonous lye.
Don't laugh. It's their National dish!
Non-Norskies can only ask why.

With any poison there's some risk,
But Norwegians are brave, and by
    dawn,
They ate all the lutafisk
And the dragon smell was gone.

A.I.

I just heard the future is 'A.I.'
Acceptive Indoctrination.
It's a psychic jab behind the eye
Producing mental castration.

Strike that! We must preserve
    decorum.
This is respectable news
From the World Economic Forum.
However, I don't share their views.

Here's A.I. in their own voices:
"First it's analytical. We snoop.
Then we nudge the dummy into
    choices.
Then we choose *for* the little dupe".

That means no elections, get it?
There's no need if we all shout "Sieg
    Heil!"

A.I. will run things, and you'll let it.
You'll be very happy. You'll smile!

It's already in your devices.
That puts you at the 'dummy' stage.
If you want to survive my advice is,
Work up some rebellious rage!

Line up your PC, phone and TV.
You're being watched through every
    screen.
Lift your leg. Make that rude noise
    for me.
They'll hear and wonder, what does
    that mean?

Now the rebellious adult
Can lay on the real zinger.
Everyone knows this insult.
Just give them the finger!

MIGRATION, THE TRUE STORY

Humans have always walked erect.
We never evolved from apes.
So let's chuck that whole aspect
And let Darwin eat sour grapes.

Let's thank the girls, make no
    mistake,
For daring to show human flair.
There was beauty even in their wake,
Unlike the gorilla's derriere.

Cave girls walking without any bend
Created a spellbinding motion
Just naturally, with their back end,
Like ripples on a calm ocean.

This charm enabled migration.
Small groups of spellbound guys
Followed them in admiration
With their feet, but more so with their
    eyes.

The girls left an unsure Eden
Rather like the Biblical tale
But they would need the guys they
    were leadin'
Risk would loom on a Biblical scale.

Fortune smiled on humankind.
They won the best parts of the Earth.
Ladies led, with men right behind,
Smiling, for whatever that's worth.

With time fashion took on a new
    trend.
Style changed to the Victorian dress.
With a huge bustle on the back end.
The girls appeared bodiless.

Men grew tired of that, by and by
And the walking roles were reversed.
But tight slacks came back which is
    why
Most guys now let ladies go first.

FREDDIE THE FIXER

They're coming for us – the IRS!
They'll have prune juice and
    handcuffs
Plus 80,000 new agents, I guess.
But is 80,000 enough?

Let's ask Freddie the Fixer,
A grizzled old mafia capo
Who put bodies in a cement mixer.
Before that he was Gestapo.

He knows the protection racket.
How to squeeze the stubborn poor.
Because even with no tax bracket
They have some pennies; you may be
    sure.

Freddie says that's a dumb question.
"Just shake 'em down", he says. But
    yikes!
Word for word here's his suggestion:

"Shoot 'em! Put their heads on
    spikes!"

Stop it Freddie! That's old time stuff.
Made me mad. I got in his face.
Times have changed! We can't be
    that rough.
I really put Freddie in his place.

I explained that I claimed zero
    income.
No blood. Cheating can be done
    gentle.
It's rigged so if IRS finds some
I can say it was accidental.

So now I'm doing 5 to 10.
Who knew? Freddie's an IRS advisor.
I should've bought protection back
    then.
In 10 years, hopefully I'm wiser.

THE CUDDLY SEA SPONGE

The adorable sea sponge is mute.
Can't speak but can leave an
 impression.
The annals of them are a hoot.
Here's a typical confession.

"I was born a helpless sea sponge.
Easy prey for starfish and slugs.
Very pretty but covered in grunge.
I needed cuddles and hugs.

Probably I'd be eaten alive.
I was destined for disaster.
I saw no way to survive.
But I was saved by a Roman Master!

My Master sniffed me for a while,
And decided to adopt me!
How I wished that I could smile!
Nothing could have stopped me.

I was put in an orphan haven

Where they could wash and hose us.
Shaggy sponges were trimmed and
 graven.
Then one by one the Masters chose
 us.

My Master is so handsome!
So admirable when he speaks.
To me he's worth a King's ransom.
And I love his rosy cheeks.

But now he shows me his lower
 parts.
I don't like that. He reeks.
He shifts his rump. He farts.
Hey! I never meant *those* cheeks!"

For politeness we'll leave it there.
The young sponge has an issue.
Not everyone got to breathe fresh air
In the days before toilet tissue.

GAIN OF FUNCTION

When I was about 10 years old
Me and my older brother
Smoked cornsilk cigars that we rolled
And got sick, first one, then the
    other.

But like researchers of today
Whose research is forbidden
We kept researching anyway
Behind a shed where we were
    hidden.

We tried weed seeds and grass
    clippings
And more substitutes, willy-nilly.
If we were caught there would be
    whippings
But young lads can get pretty silly.

'Macho' was the main idea.
Survival was the main thought.

We quit when we got diarrhea
Which led to us being caught.

So there. That's my confession.
We were messing with 'Gain-of-
    Function'.
I'll never forget Dad's expression.
He taught us the meaning of
    compunction.

My story's sort of like Wuhan.
And their Gain-of-Function
    experiments.
They gave the world a lot to chew on.
With no remorse, just arrogance.

Their next bug might be worse than
    covid
By five or even ten-fold.
They really ought to quit like we did
When we were only 10 years old.

ISHI'S TROLL POT

We must preserve our ecology!
This is our only planet.
Save the species! Make no apology!
Even those underground made of
    granite.

Wait – what? Species should be alive.
Yes, and that includes the great
    trolls.
They're from stone and big ones
    survive
Down below all our sinkholes.

Ishi, the witch, is their mother.
She paints them on a deep cavern
    wall
With paint from a pot like no other.
Some are over 10 feet tall.

But unfortunately for the race
They're all boys. She can only paint
    guys.
One can tell by the uglier face
And she wakes them by lighting their
    eyes.

Her pot hangs under a drip
From a toxic pool far above
Where deformed frogs skinny-dip.
This is Ishi's labor of love.

It's her critical habitat.
Our zoning laws mustn't forget her!
If this grumpy little dingbat
Needs that yuck to paint trolls, we
    must let her!

Her trolls are stuck in that wall
Til she invites them out. She could.
But Ishi is not nice at all
And neither are most of her brood.

First she tests their loyalty,
Offering her hand like a Queen or
    King
Because she sees herself as Royalty.
And she loves when the brutes kiss
    her ring.

FACT CHECKERS

Knights of the internet! Or so they
    dream.
Except for God their word is highest.
Check that. Online they're supreme!
But unlike God, they're biased.

They're like that King who wore no
    clothes
Except they have mouths on both
    ends,
Interchangeable as everyone knows,
So whatever comes out offends.

That's a sure way to ruin the game,
Being a biased umpire.

And they do it for money. Shame!
I rate an honest hooker much higher.

Fact checkers were known to the
    cavemen
As busybodies on the grapevine.
They were called 'scuttlebutts' then,
Known by an obvious sign.

Scuttlebutts were vegetarian,
All of them, without a doubt.
They couldn't even chew carrion
Because their teeth had been
    knocked out.

RENEWABLE FUELS

Pity the poor Ice Age tribe
When they heard the glaciers
    rending,
Crushing trees, sending horrible
    vibes
What to do? Was the world ending?

The Chief, a wise socialite
Caught the vibes and lashed out in
    fear,
"We must stop burning wood –
    tonight!
Or the trees will be gone in one
    year".

The good people rallied, aghast,
Except one dummy who voiced
    concern.
He said glaciers don't move that fast.
And anyway, what would we burn?

The Chief replied, "Mammoth poop!
Because it's so renewable".
He convinced everyone but the stupe
That one month would prove it was
    doable.

They burned no wood that autumn
    night.

By morning they were all cold.
So they scrounged all about the
    campsite
For what the Chief called 'Brown
    Gold".

He cheered them on from where he
    stood.
They all scrounged, socialites too.
But to say no more, an armload of
    wood
Smelled better than an armload of
    poo.

Next month the stupe was hanged as
    a denier.
For making an ice-speed graph
Which showed the Chief was a liar.
The ice moved just an inch and a
    half.

The tribe went back to wood-
    gathering
Which seemed a better solution.
People smiled and the Chief started
    blathering
About mammoth poop pollution.

MEDICAL WATER PRESSURE

The old Chief was bound up again.
Some blockage deep in the derriere.
And the tribe suffered with him when
He needed that kind of healthcare.

Maybe it was too much mammoth
    steak.
Something stubborn was in his route.
He complained and for everyone's
    sake
The tribe wished he could force it
    out.

The Shaman offered to help
But the old Chief didn't comprehend.
A glass of water just made him yelp:
"The trouble's at the other end!"

Then the human race showed its
    stuff.

Oog and some other fellows
Got the Chief to strip down to the
    buff
And employed a home-made bellows.

Using warm water and a tube
And pumping the bellows many-a,
They injected enough harmless lube
To achieve the world's first enema!

Thus human medicine advanced
But Oog will need a refresher.
Poor Oog. Imagine how he danced
In that blast of internal pressure.

Masks and gowns were non-existent
And the release happens quite fast.
Now Oog has a surgical assistant
To stand in the way of the blast.

THE FANNYSTONE

Let us have peace! May good will
    abound!
Between the stone trolls and
    mankind.
Please don't kick big rocks in the
    ground
They could be a stone troll's behind.

Kids might cause this kind of danger.
They will poke sticks into crannies
That belong to giant strangers
Who don't want that up their fannies!

The child might still be okay
If the sun is shining bright.
Trolls stay underground by day.

But that one will be out tonight.

It's probably the one called Gump.
He's quiet. He doesn't snore.
He has the biggest, hardest rump.
So he usually plugs their door.

He also has the best nose,
The worst temper, and he's smart.
He'll track you tonight, I suppose,
And he'll tear your house apart!

Haha! They leave humans alone.
That was just my little joke.
It tickles my funny bone.
Go ahead, give him another poke.

SMILODON'S DOWNFALL

He didn't greet Sammi on the
    causeway
But Smilodon was straight ahead.
He would leap at the new human
    prey.
Cavemen or lions would all end up
    dead.

Smiley was the apex carnivore
With those horrible fangs.
The T-Rex of his day. He loved gore
And had constant hunger pangs.

Old T-Rex was just bloody and dull
While Smiley's approach was
    surgical.
He could disembowel or puncture
    your skull.
But both of them were unmerciful.

So how could Sammi and friends
    survive?
With flesh of such juicy uniqueness?
I think our brain kept us alive.
Smilodon had a weakness.

Cavemen grunted then, trying to
    make sense,
Before teachers made our words
    crisp.
But beastly speech was even worse,
    no offense.
And Smilodon had an accent. A lisp.

He loved to gloat when he cornered
    men.
But men asked, when the lisp
    appeared,
"Pardon me – what was that again?
And when Smilodon paused he got
    speared.

MAMMOTHS

I know the fate of the Mammoth
    herds
But to learn the secret behind it,
Think jewelry fashion. In other
    words,
Cave girls! That's where you'll find it.

In those days the earth was
    harmonious.
There were predators and there was
    prey.
No one was sanctimonious
Because every dog had its day.

Sabretooth necklaces changed that.
Though mammoth herds were
    immense
Each time men killed a sabretooth
    cat
The herds grew bigger. Just common
    sense.

Each cat had a pair of tooth
    "pendants",
And girlfriends loved that get-up.
Which led to weddings and
    descendants.
It starts to add up, Buttercup.

In a few thousand years the
    scoreboard
Showed very few big cats remained,
While mammoth numbers soared.
But why had ambient temperature
    gained?

Because mammoths blew out the
    methane charts…
(As I search for presentable words)
From their burps and (rhymes with
    darts)
Which is gas without (rhymes with
    birds).

By doubling and tripling in size
The herds blasted so much
    greenhouse gas
It warmed earth and assured their
    demise
That's quite a kick in their (rhymes
    with class).

So let's credit cave girl sweethearts
For tipping that domino.
To assure enough mammoth farts,
The sabretooths had to go.

FOOTPRINTS

Utah is a place for throwbacks
Where the wind blows timeless sands
That scour up human tracks
From the Ice Age, from old wetlands.

Tracks of beasts are crossing or
	meeting,
Probably made the same day
Since weather conditions are fleeting
And rain could have washed them
	away.

As we follow the human tracks,
Of a Mom, and let's say her
	daughter,

Were beasts stalking behind their
	backs?
Will we come to a scene of slaughter?

If Mom was searching for a better life
Would her dreams soon prove
	hollow?
We must hope she had a sharp knife!
But guess what? The beasts didn't
	follow.

That's our earliest look at the luck
That always made America glow.
The Old World doesn't have it. They
	suck.
But we've always had get-up-and-go!

SUNDALAND

We should ask of those footprints in
time
Where were you walking from?
Since the Ice Age was still in its
prime,
From where might you have come?

Humans know boats, you must
agree.
Could they have sailed from Siberia?
Doubtful. There was ice up there in
the sea.
So that won't meet the criteria.

We must look past China to the south
Since our Native Tribes weren't
Chinese,
To the Sundaland. There's word of
mouth
That they explored all the warm seas.

The Polynesians set sail first of all.
Their girls were gorgeous. They were
beauties.
They held the whole ocean in their
thrall
And danced with grass skirts on their
booties.

Other Sundaland guys were obsessed

And set out to win the beauties back.
They had the caveman clubs girls
detest
And could win any girl with one
whack.

The Polynesian men were no match,
Being soft from easy island life,
So most girls were easy to catch
And became some caveman's wife.

The others fled out of fear
And discovered Ecuador.
They were the only humans here.
But then the cave dudes arrived
offshore.

From there the tale is less clear.
It was a strong El Nino year
So the westerlies brought them all
here,
Where they just seemed to disappear.

Intermarriage changed 'em
thenceforth,
Except she who walked the white
sands.
She escaped and made her way north
And married a nice Cro-Magnan
man.

CAVE PAINTING

Did cavemen have a human heart?
Did they show humanity at play?
They painted animals, and that's art,
But it's not human nature, per se.

Maybe art speaks to the soul.
But that's not what I'm after, sweetie.
Humans are playful, on the whole,
So where is their graffiti?

Let's ask an archeologist
If he's awake. Rock art is a bore.
It's been seen. Nothing's been
    missed.
There's old Sam! Oh, let's just let
    him snore.

These paintings here were first
    shown
In an encyclopedia.
Now you can scroll them on your
    phone.
They're boring, even on mass media.

Because good art and good paint
    were rare
Graffiti artists used cowpies.
Which didn't help the cavern air

But it's gone. It flakes off when it
    dries.

The question is, did it leave a trace?
Are cave walls like a computer file?
Is deleted data on the rock face?
Let's run a high-tech trial.

For this we'll use infrared light
Which should reveal, when the wall is
    scanned
The deleted stuff – there it is, alright.
On a less-tasteful band.

Hmm. Rude pics and … must be
    comments.
I can only guess at the words.
Dirty limericks with caveman
    accents?
Anyhow, I can see they weren't
    nerds.

We've recovered Ice Age cyber trash!
If it was paper they would've burned
    it.
Shall we show Sam our cyber cache?
Nah. Sleeping Beauty never earned
    it.

THE CHARM

Creation was the Lord's job, although
Celestial quilters had a duty
To add a feminine touch, to sew
Smooth edges and bestow beauty.

The Artisans of Evermore!
So jovial, yet genteel
Used threads of light in days of yore,
But their needles were sharp and real.

But needles break, as anyone knows
And they toted bagsful along.
Then opportunity arose
Pixies wanted them! What could go
    wrong?

So they heard the pixies' sob story.
The Lord's rule was, they should
    ignore it.
It was heart-wrenching, bloody and
    gory

But they knew the pixies asked for it.

Pixies did tease trolls with bravado
But there was no place on earth to
    hide,
Thus many a small desperado
Had been eaten. They're good batter
    fried.

They were so full of remorse!
And promises to apologize!
They would behave better, of course!
Not one of them had dry eyes.

So the Artisans helped their young
    friends
And sewed charmed needles into the
    bushes.
But pixies never did make amends
So the charm was pulled off their
    tushes.

THE ORACLE ON THE MOUNT

The Oracle was still young
On his Tibetan mountaintop
When the communists cut out his
    tongue
For telling the truth, non-stop.

In fairness it was all he knew
Except commies don't like excuses.
But the rest of him was like brand-
    new,
Perhaps he could find new uses.

The best place, as everyone knows,
To start afresh is the USA.
At least that's where everyone goes.
You can walk right in any day.

What jobs are there for migrants?
Just the cheap ones? Are you sure?
Great jobs should line up in advance
For a guy who can tell the future!

No! They have guys, Hi-Tech
    bosses,
Who know if you'll make a good
    geek.
They know losers and all the causes.
They don't want someone who can't
    speak.

But wait! Hold up with your pity.
The Oracle found an upside!
He got out of the city
And found work as a fishing guide.

He always knew where the fish
    would be
Like most guides can only wish.
And guides don't talk very much,
    sweet pea.
That's a no-no. It scares the fish.

DUE PROCESS

Did cavemen ever raise their voices?
Were there arguments, petty crime?
Tribal justice did offer choices
But money talked every time.

A plaintiff would plead his case
Then witnesses stepped up. It's
    funny,
Like most of the human race
They always sided with the money.

That was back in the Ice Age.
When Due Process was just evolving.
When lawyers worked for minimum
    wage
But got cash for problem-solving.

In time, simple witness counts,
Which had been so easy to rig,
And for piddling amounts,

Were swapped for juries. That was
    big!

There would be juries of their peers!
Finally. Employees who'd been
    cheated
And downtrodden for years
Could get their buddies seated.

Happy ending? No! A clever lawyer
With money and plausible denial
Could flip any jury for the employer
And turn it into a mistrial.

One day they would invent the
    'appeal'.
But you'll need deep pockets, honey.
The poor are just doomed to a crappy
    deal.
It's very hard to beat the money.

THE MICE

The Lord appointed his bright-eyed
    birds –
Ix, the sun and Oolwa, the moon
"To light the earth by turn" were His
    words.
Then He left, but He left too soon.

Ix had the daylight hours,
Or should have. Owl had the night.
Both overreached their assigned
    powers.
Which led to a rip-roaring fight.

The skies blazed and oceans tossed.
Each put out an eye of their rival.

They fought to a draw and the cost
Was a boom in mouse survival.

A single eye meant lots of shadow,
And we are paying the price.
Without a good binocular glow
The birds couldn't catch the mice.

But times change. Today business
    loves mice.
There are products. Your phone will
    have apps.
Buy them! Let's beat the mice at any
    price.
And we will, until they outlaw traps.

HAG FLIES

Do you have flies in your house?
Lots of dust that's hard to get rid of?
Complaints about this from a
    spouse?
A subconscious urge to wear gloves?

You may be harboring a Night Hag.
She's hibernating, but your flies
They're working for the old nag.
Her thought is in them. They're her
    eyes.

The rest of her sleeps in the dust
While her eyes study the occupants.
You must take my word for this.
    Have trust!
There are no actual documents.

It might take years. Hags are pretty
    dumb.
And flies are short-lived. So what
    then?
Hag flies simply clone themselves
    from
Bathroom mirrors, again and again.

For the Hag though, it's scary.
House garbage flies are pretty cute.
If her true flies and those intermarry
Her chances of rebirth are moot.

So bring your smelly garbage inside.
Flies too! Well, you likely brought
    'em.
Or if you're nervous that I just lied
Find the true Hag Flies and swat
    'em.

DIRE WOLVES

Is it the size of the fight in the dog,
Or the size of the dog in the fight?
Doesn't matter in an asphalt bog.
La Brea was a horrible sight.

Thirst must have played some part.
Water puddles likely fooled the first
    beast.
Tar trapped any who were less than
    smart,
Like Dire Wolves, who rushed out to
    feast.

They've excavated some tar pits.
Come see the wolf skulls! They're
    ghoulish.
That species surely had the least
    wits.
But lots of beasts were foolish.

The tar pits were nature's IQ test.
Evolution sort of works that way.
Dire wolf packs once were the best
But our world would not be their day.

They would come to our asphalt
    highways
Drawn to road kill by old instinct.
Trucks would hit them all in a few
    days.
Dire Wolves were meant to be
    extinct.

Tour guides keep a daily scoreboard.
What species? How many? A rolling
    sum.
But one species has been ignored.
No cavemen were ever that dumb.

BLANK SHEETS OF PAPER

There are no protests in China.
Or the video doesn't get out.
Either way the Commies kinda
Slam the lid. There's no room for
    doubt.

We might hear of it – but no pics.
I wish I had pics for this one.
Some people think peasants are hicks
But the Chinese are genius at puns.

They should be. They've had
    complaints
Since paper and chalk were invented.
Through centuries of Royal
    constraints
They've made posters and bitched
    and vented.

To no avail. It's gotten worse.
Now the Commies are banning
All posters, chapter and verse,
And the spy cameras are scanning.

No slogans! No messages allowed!
What would you do if all speech was
    banned?
The Chinese still form a crowd
And this is funny! Very well planned:

They wave posters with sarcasm
In a fierce, unpunishable caper.
They taunt old Xi, give him a spasm,
Waving thousands of sheets of blank
    paper.

Magna Charta

The notion that others had rights
Outside of the Royal Family
Like barons maybe, or their knights
Still awaited a Royal Decree.

That changed on the field of
    Runnymede
In England. That was all parta
When King John was forced to
    concede
And signed the Magna Charta.

Barons wrote that document
Demanding rights they had never
    got.
Democracy is what they meant
They didn't get that, but they got a
    lot.

Church rights would be protected.
Lower taxes were of the essence.
The barons would be respected.
The text did not mention peasants.

Baron's rights filled half the page.
It was blank on the bottom half.
Peasant's rights must wait for a New
    Age.
The Nobles ignored the riffraff.

The blank half was thrown away.
Angry peasants found it and saved it.
Like the Chinese would do someday,
They defied their Masters and waved
    it.

THE PRINTING PRESS

When word of the Gutenberg Bible
And a much lower price for books
Reached the Royals they knew they
    were liable
For trouble with janitors and cooks.

Times had changed since the Ice
    Age.
Royals had alphabets and scrolls.
All this knowledge in a written
    language
They kept to themselves, the arse -
    (rhymes with moles).

It was hard for the unwashed masses
To succeed in the rigged game.
Such was life for lads and lasses
Who couldn't even spell their name.

But now! With cheap books going
    global

And education replacing hearsay
Peasants could be upward mobile.
At last! The breaks were going their
    way.

Though still unable to change what
    was
They could read up on what should
    be.
That's what the printing press does.
It showed the poor what could be.

That 'could be' really would be
    someday
Though the Royals burned books to
    stall it.
The American Dream was on the
    way.
"All men are equal", we call it.

JACK FROST

Trees are very residuous.
Set in their ways. Thick skinned.
But lots of them turned deciduous
After the Winter of the North Wind.

That was the first really cold one.
When the Ice Queen had grown
    strong.
Trees knew when that winter was
    done
They must change to survive winters
    that long.

Imps, spirits of the trees, complained
To a Captain of the North, Jack
    Frost.
"The Queen likes this", he
    explained.
So change your ways or you're lost".

But Jack liked the little imps.
"Lose your sap", he advised. "Take
    up art.
Tease the Queen with graffiti, you
    shrimps!
No time like the present to start".

They did take up art, painting leaves
And ridiculous Queens, in frost
    crystals.
It's all over your windows and eaves
Since they invented water pistols.

Word of all this reached Her
    Highness
And she promptly fired Jack.
His loss would prove a big minus.
But you can bet that *she'll* be back.

THE MAN IN THE MOON

Do you see the Man in the Moon?
At one time it might have been so.
He awakened each day around noon
And watched the human race grow.

Now in our imaginations
We might see parts of a face.
But not in the right locations.
And the eyes are all over the place.

One theory is, the Great Spirit
Set the man up at creation
With the earth and the moon just
    near it,
As an eavesdropping station.

The moon slept through some of the
    previews
Amoebas, beasts and their downfall.

Let's forgive him for a little snooze.
He did shine on them all.

Finally humans, as you expect.
Cave people, then the Chosen Ones.
They were all sinners, less than
    perfect.
Same with their daughters and sons.

It confused the Man in the Moon.
Had he waited so long for *this?*
We disappointed him so soon!
The best of us were hit or miss.

It got worse. Slavery and wars.
The Man in the Moon turned around.
His butt has some pimples and sores
And that's what we see from the
    ground.

PLUTO SPEAKS OUT

The planet Pluto cooled off quite
   early
But alien forms had become great.
Then in the cool-down, slowly but
   surely,
They morphed into a mental state.

We found Pluto around 1930
And labelled it 'Planet Nine'.
It looped the sun, looked fairly sturdy
And everything was fine.

Now the IAU, whoever they are,
Have re-labelled it a dwarf runt,
And broadcast this insult so far
The Plutonians heard the affront.

Earth got a phone call, a bombshell.
From Pluto. On the line was Janet,
An angry Plutonian demoiselle
Annoyed at the term 'dwarf planet'.

Janet went on to demand
That earthlings take back that word!

This was broadcast world-wide, every
   band.
When she paused Billy Ray called her
   a turd.

Earthlings laughed, for what it's
   worth,
But Janet had an icy warning:
By noon they would come and fry the
   earth!
And it was already morning.

They could teleport at light speed.
That gave us just five hours.
It was all the time we would need
If we used all our broadcast powers

How to stop them? What should we
   beam?
They were mental. What's like
   mental prunes?
Think outside the box. Think goofy
   scheme.
We saved earth! We beamed Far Side
   cartoons.

FERMENTED GRAPES

Who really discovered alcohol?
It was birds first, and then Little Ben.
They both ate fermented grapes,
    LOL.
Ben was a 10 year old cave boy then.

The heart of an ornithologist
Beat in him, as he watched birds eat
    grapes.
So he ate some too. Who could resist?
Benny wasn't much smarter than
    apes.

But pioneers aren't always smart.
Ideas can come out of the blue.
Yes, the birds had a head start
But soon Benny was falling down
    too.

His Mom found him and scolded
"Dear boy! What were you thinking?"
Too late. A new sin had unfolded.
Ben had kicked off the Age of
    Drinking.

That's still going on even now.
I've been there too, and I had
    warning.
Evenings were a blast but holy cow!
You pay for it the next morning.

But how much beer, or spirits or
    wine
Is a problem with Saint Peter?
I do worry. If I cross the line,
Could I work my sins off as a greeter?

BABOONS

A message to anthropologists:
Use your monkey skulls for spittoons!
We are not monkey cousins. Case
  dismissed.
But had you thought about baboons?

Like us they live in social groups.
Like us some have lice and fleas.
Like (homeless) us they scatter
  poops.
Unlike us they sleep sitting in trees.

We could too now and not get sore.
Our backsides have evolved a bit
  plump.

If you've never seen baboons before
They have the same useful rump.

Like ours, there's cushy layers upon
  it.
So cushy it sort of protrudes.
One day they'll put a surtax on it
Because it comes from very rich
  foods.

We're like baboons, anatomically.
What more proof do you need, my
  friend?
Fossils are cool, but comically,
Anthropologists study the wrong end.

THE BEAR DIET

Thermometers weren't invented
So the Ice Age was measured in
  groans.
But the cavemen were contented.
By August they had fat on their
  bones.

Thanks to bears they found honey.
For that favor they didn't hunt bears.
Bees didn't think this was funny.
But you can't talk to bees – so who
  cares?

So cavemen dieted like bears
And got fat - first choice, then prime.
But while bears hibernate in lairs
Men hunted all the time.

With a honeycomb bag lunch
Cavemen could hunt all day.
They speared mammoths, that's my
  hunch.

But spring was a long ways away.

The seasons were different then:
Winter, winter, more winter, then
  spring.
While the bear slept in his den
Humans suffered through
  everything.

By spring starvation was lurking
And cavemen were worse for the
  wear.
If evolution was working
Which species should go on from
  there?

Counting downtime those bears were
  wimps
And by comparison, sleazier.
Evolution knew it in a glimpse.
But those bears sure had it easier.

SIDEWINDERS

Did the Great Spirit make
    rattlesnakes?
I doubt it. They just slithered in
From the Darkness. That's all it takes
So that's how it's always been.

What the Great Spirit did do was
He banished the worst ones
To the dry quarters of earth because
Good folks did not yet have guns.

He hung rattles on the snake's bum
So good folk would know where
    they're at
Which became a rule of thumb,
An alarm, like belling the cat.

Sounds good, huh? But no such luck.
For those who need reminders

These are the snakes that really suck.
And the very worst were sidewinders.

No one volunteered, for what that's
    worth,
To be a cop out there, if
It was the last place on earth.
So crime prospered without a sheriff.

Great Spirit reworded His ad
Leaving out 'gentler' and 'kinder'.
Impatient, He punched on His
    keypad:
Who can straighten out a sidewinder?

It was a bit crass, but that done 'er.
Roadrunners signed up two by two.
They're a wacky bunch who were
Collectively known as the 'Cuckoo'.

GRIMPER

Way back in geological time
There was one landmass, called
    Pangea.
It was bound up due to a crime
And the mass needed diarrhea.

Grimper had Pangea in his grip.
The great vine was 'Captain of the
    Boat'.
He was rooted so deeply amidship
That Pangea couldn't break up and
    float.

Eventually Mother Nature
Became aware of what was amiss.
Great Spirit was busy, she felt sure,
So she had to make sense of this.

She stopped the rain, which withered
    all plants.

Soon Grimper, Captain of Pangea,
Was only Captain of the ants.
Then he croaked, a still better idea.

The parched ground where he grew
Baked in the hot sun and cracked.
The great landmass split in two
And then seven parts, to be exact.

They're the continents we know
    today
That once were in serious doubt.
So let's just be thankful, hey?
For that one really good drought.

All that could never happen now.
Sleep well tonight. Have no fear!
Grimper was a weed anyhow
And our gardeners have pruning
    shears.

THE BEST WAR

The best war? Is there such a thing?
It depends on how you rate them.
Like 'good' when they got rid of a
    king,
Not so good when their enemies ate
    them.

In the war over Helen of Troy
The booty haul was near zero.
Except of course for one boy.
I think Helen married the hero.

World War 1 wasn't best, just dumb.
An Archduke got shot, so millions
    died.
Are there more Dukes where he came
    from?
Let's shoot them now to be on the
    safe side.

World War 2 gave us the atom bomb.
I guess that's best for the winning
    side.
But like Korea and Viet Nam,
For no good reason millions died.

Genghis Khan built a pyramid of
    skulls.

That's the best architectural war.
Such splendor! But only til seagulls
Messed it up with their morning
    chore.

The American Civil War
Could be best if every slaver
Mustered up in their own army corps
And got beat. That would be a favor.

The wars of European Royals
Were impressive, but too long.
There'd be nothing left for spoils.
One hundred year wars are just
    wrong.

The best wars were the Crusades.
Even though millions died.
And probably some went to Hades
But they all felt God was on their
    side.

If there are different Gods under the
    sun
For both Islam and Christianity
That might work, but if there's just
    one
I think He would question our sanity.

THE DOLLS

It's good to live in these centuries.
The old days were so full of bias.
They sent poor folks to penitentiaries
And burned witches for not being
    pious.

They burned 'em all, girls and old
    nags
On tips from anonymous snitches.
Most were innocent, some were
    Night Hags
But they never got the real witches.

For the innocents their only crime
Was living in that millennium.
But witchcraft is cool at the present
    time
In our own inclusive biennium.

Witches are coming out everywhere.
They're really doing outreach.
Fight them! But use silent prayer
Or you might be charged with hate
    speech.

Yet they still reach in vain for love
And they don't look good on TV.
It would help if they coo' d like a
    dove
Instead of a banshee.

I think they're headed for Hades
After their last curtain call.
But the Devil's Own Lovely Ladies
Have a sweet acronym: They're the
    DOLLS.

JOAN-OF-ARC

What would you do if you heard
    voices
Saying, "Fight the bloody English!
    Hark!"
I did fight that class, but we had no
    choices.
But then, I'm no Joan-of-Arc.

Anyhow, she claimed she heard
    Saints
And went before the King to implore,
Would he waive the girl-soldier
    restraints?
And the King sent her off to war.

She arrived with colors flying
And in no time the Brits were rattled.
Joan-of-Arc hadn't been lying
And the Englishmen skedaddled.

She saved the French at Orleans,
Inspired victories and laughter.
All this while still in her teens!
But things went haywire thereafter.

She was captured and burned as a
    witch
And was named as a Saint by the
    Pope.
Joan-of-Arc had a world-shaking itch.
But she never took time to skip rope.

To be a Saint you should die first.
Joan did that when still teenage.
For myself, since it can't be reversed,
I would like it to be from old age.

TYRANNOSAURUS LIPS

We thought we knew T-Rex well.
Turns out we were missing a clue.
He had lips from the opening bell.
Lips like us! If we only knew.

That changes everything. Rex could
    speak!
Hollywood must turn down the roar.
I wouldn't say they were meek.
But they kissed! Prove me wrong.
    And there's more.

Girl T-Rexes withheld their charms.
Holding hands was mostly their
    druthers.

But when they held hands with short
    arms
Their lips bumped into each other's.

There it is. The first kiss in history.
Before even Adam and Eve.
Probably bloody and blistery.
But they were beasts, young and
    naïve.

That kiss launched the Romantic
    Age.
The kiss itself is now more refined.
The girl's goal is to become engaged.
The boy is momentarily blind.

LEECHES

It's a fact. Doctors still use leeches.
Not so much tho, like years ago.
The French loved them, so tales
    teach us.
When did this start? Does anyone
    know?

The Ice Age would be the best guess.
A shaman would have his clinic
For tribal members in distress
And leeches would be a great
    gimmick.

He would start treating a headache
By employing upbeat speeches.
Then, trying hard not to look fake,
He applied bloodsucking leeches.

He used them nine times out of ten.
But it did leave quite a mess.

There was lots of cleanup, but then
Who could argue with success?

Most pains go away anyhow
So leeches were a moneymaker.
He charged all the market would
    allow
And was also the undertaker.

But the kids who captured the worms
Went on strike for better pay
And before he could come to terms
Folks learned that most pains *do* go
    away.

The leech fad was a hoax
But people with money will still pay.
So some kids and some poor folks
Still make a few bucks every day.

FACT CHECKERS #2

We know what fact-checkers are
    there for.
They're partisan. That's the fuss.
When we know this they become a
    bore.
But they could help all of us.

They need to expand their
    awareness.
There's fake posts all over Facebook.
Just in the interest of fairness,
Wake up and take a look!

Aliens are a favorite theme.
We've all heard of UFO's,
Or laughed at UFO memes,
"Cause we knew they were fake, I
    suppose.

Used to be I could spot A.I. pics.
They were always…*off*…somehow.
But the bots have achieved a nice fix.
They've got everything perfect now.

So I still spot the A.I. pics.
They're *too* perfect. So's the caption.
Humans aren't perfect. Not even the
    chicks.
But they are in A.I. adaption.

This should be stopped. Fact-
    checkers should scream.
If they really *were* know-it-alls
They would do this as a team!
But alas, they have no baseballs.

RAIDING FOR WOMEN

Ah, the good old days of tough
    cavemen!
There was no divorce back in the
    day.
Men did whatever they pleased, and
    then,
Wives who complained were traded
    away!

Grumpy men from different tribes
Went to swap meets with unhappy
    wives.
Because some marriages just had
    bad vibes.
And this did save some husband's
    lives.

This was all done without tears.
To save face men called them raids.

But the wives were all volunteers
And called most of the shots for the
    trades.

If you were there you'd be impressed.
Men were washed, girls had nice
    hairdos.
All the grumps tried to look their
    best.
But some trades needed bribes and
    booze.

All the 'raiders' went home with new
    wives,
Quit washing, quit wearing
    suspenders.
And the gals started sharpening
    knives.
They were all repeat offenders.

CHAIN GANGS

When the beasts were gone, the cavemen
Turned to gardening and farming.
No longer idolized as brave men
Some turned to drink, which was alarming.

About half the guys got lazy
And the lazy ones got fat too.
It drove the working people crazy.
Then came thievery. It's all true.

You would think the village Chief
Would stop this. He should be the dude.
But he was as fat as any thief
And he helped them steal food.

The good folks worked from dawn to sunset.
They perspired and they smelled.
Just the men – I don't think girls sweat.
Then one day they all rebelled.

There was a brawl, but it was short.
The lazy bums were out of shape.
They were charged with a lot of tort.
The Chief too. He didn't escape.

They weren't locked up and fed
And no one wanted them to hang
So they were put to work instead.
These bums made up the first chain gang.

PAPYRUS

If you want to hear angry voices,
Frustrated people trapped in doubt,
Give us existential choices
Between two things we can't live
    without!

Our toughest choice was that apple,
    hey?
But when they invented papyrus
We gave writing paper an 'A'
But toilet tissue got an 'A' Plus.

An industry sprang into being
But which was the most pressing
    issue?
Well, we do more than just (rhymes
    with skiing)
So they prioritized toilet tissue.

Soon there were six grades to choose
    from.
Pharoah bought all the Number
    Ones.

Since he had a sensitive bum.
The Queen too, but she called that
    her buns.

Unscrupulous craftsmen appeared
And made the tissue thin and
    narrow..
Doggone fingers poked through and
    smeared.
Luckily, that wasn't Pharoah.

It was poor folks, like monks.
Their fingers poked through, made
    holes.
They wiped them on their under
    trunks.
And that isn't all ink on their scrolls.

That could happen to you today
Following your own toilet caper.
We no longer have Pharaohs, hooray!
But your government gets the best
    paper.

TELEPROMPTERS

How smart is your politician,
Or any that you may have known?
I don't mean their ambition.
I mean, can they speak on their own?

The more they're a-barking and
    baying
The more this should matter.
Do they even know what they're
    saying?
Or is it teleprompter chatter?

Other times they're so smooth and
    glib
But they don't show the prompter
    screen.
Let's pull the plug and make them
    ad-lib.

They don't know what half words
    mean.

But someone does. Their puppet
    master.
They ghost write those words that
    sound so fair.
They're smarter and their plans move
    faster
If a puppet reads them on the air.

For proper motivation, LOL,
So the puppet is feeling his oats
I've heard they prime 'em with
    Adderall
In order to win more votes.

CUPID

To make sure love blossomed in
    Eden
The Great Spirit put Cupid there too,
And before that apple was eaten
Cupid did what he was sent to do.

His love arrow had a golden tip
And he nicked Eve! This was
    unrehearsed.
It should have sparked human
    courtship.
But she saw the apple first.

She so wanted it! But she was
    nervous.
A snake offered it. Was it perverse?
She gave it to Adam, a disservice.
He took a bite, but it was a curse.

Too bad Cupid used that arrow.
He had another that produced a
    snub.
That one had a tip of lead.
It would have foiled Beelzebub.

Or – what would have been worse,
He could've winged Adam with the
    lead.
No courtship, no kids, just a curse.
Whoa! Gotta get that outa my head!

How much nicer for those rookies,
If the devil hadn't been there.
There could've been wedding cake
    and cookies
And a honeymoon, and daycare.

ICE AGE FED

Most Ice Age folk were cold, but
    happy.
Nights were frosty but most days
    were sunny.
People smiled without being sappy.
And then they discovered money.

Some traveler had cowry shells
And explained what they were worth.
He worked for the Ice Age cartels
-I mean *banks*- They were new on
    earth.

It created quite a stir.
Folks scrambled, even raided
    dowries.
He walked out of there with the
    finest fur.
And all for just a few cowries.

The Chief had a private pow-wow
About where to go? How to borrow?
How much collateral for now?
The guy said, "Come with me
    tomorrow".

You know what's next. For a lower
    rate
He borrowed bags of cowry cash.
Which he then loaned out times
    about eight
And nobody batted an eyelash.

They all planned to buy groceries
    cheap
And some furs too, and some honey!
But inflation had shot up steep.
They had to borrow money.

They found that they couldn't afford
Any more than they used to,
And when interest came due – oh
    Lord!
It added up! They had let it accrue.

It was good to be Village Chief.
He foreclosed on a lot of loans.
Folks started calling him a thief,
But businessmen must ignore
    groans.

Someday bigger Chiefs would say,
"You'll own nothing and be happy!"
But folks weren't quite there yet, that
    day.
They owned nothing, yes, but felt
    crappy.

They went and built a new town for
    themselves
That had no bank, but children rang
    bells.
Pretty soon they all had food on their
    shelves
While the old Chief chewed his cowry
    shells.

FLASH MOBS

Here's a new one for you: Flash
    mobs!
Gangs of thieves loot rich stores on
    cue.
Just bums that don't have any jobs.
It happened in Old England too.

Their thieves all looked alike – just
    slobby.
With snotty kerchiefs on their faces.
Way too many for any Bobbie,
So they just let 'em loot rich places.

Well, most stores had only cheap
    stuff.
London Town was slummy back
    when.
But one day the rich folk had
    enough.
Bobbies almost got fired, and then…

A whole flash mob was caught.
A bunch of neighborhood youth.
They roughed 'em up good, as they
    ought
Until they admitted the truth.

Then someone remembered a rope
And while citizens cursed and
    danged 'em
And the young lads lost all hope
Authorities prepared to hang 'em.

But the Bobbies held out to just jail
    'em
To go easy on the young pups.
"They're just kids. It's easy to nail
    'em.
We'd rather hang some Higher-Ups".

Machu Picchu

It's the story of the human race.
The more we change the more we're
    the same.
The Incas had a privileged place
Like our Davos, just a different
    name.

The exclusive Machu Picchu!
Reserved for pampered Royal
    presence.
Plus some elites, so just those few
Could Lord it over the peasants.

Royals were descended from the sun
So the Emperor built this lavish lair.
It was over the top when it was done.

But hey, they had to Lord it from
    somewhere!

One day - hurrah! – here come the
    Spanish.
They conquered it all without much
    cost.
The Inca Royalty vanished
And their cool vacation place was
    lost.

We need conquistadors at Davos
To rid us of those Big Shots and
    shills.
I think we would get lots of 'Bravos',
But then we'd have to pay their bills.

GENIE IN A BOTTLE

If you find a bottle like these
You won't know. It just shows size
    and weight
Plus deposit and retail fees
And of course an expiration date.

But study the ingredients.
Genies are mostly hot air.
It will look empty, that's common
    sense,
But I tell you, he's actually there.

Rub the bottle. Don't shake it!
It's best if he's in a good mood.
And heaven help you if you break it,
Or you'll be stuck with him, dude.

So – Poof! – Here he is. Could be
    worse.
It's a five hundred dollar one.
He's got that much in his purse.
But you can't wish for the money,
    Hon.

You'll get 3 wishes, but you must
Keep the value under five hundred.
If you go over, you go bust,
And prices are up if you've wondered.

Want a kiss from some movie star?
Her time is money, that's the trouble.
A real one costs too much by far
But you might get a cheap stunt
    double.

Oh, one more thing. Genie wants his
    cut.
That's 50 percent off the top.
Plus tax, shipping, tips, tut-tut.
You just broke even. It's a swap.

So stuff your genie back inside.
You were born too late the way it
    looks.
Your genie isn't bona fide
Like the ones in story books.

SMOKE SIGNALS

Before cavemen had formal speech
Or a written language was defined
They discovered their smoke could
    reach
Other tribes, who replied in kind.

The reply launched a New Age.
Tribes refined and tailored their
    smoke
To show thoughts like a written
    page:
A language for illiterate folk!

It opened up the Long Distance Call
But Shamans saw possible downside
As bad as home-brewed alcohol,
So the new 'grapevine' was denied.

Kids used it anyhow.
Progress must find a way
Or we'd still be cavemen, even now,
And the grapevine did seem okay.

Taming fire had put us up on beasts.

Now this was like frosting on our
    cakes.
But the Shamans and their priests
Still tried to put on the brakes.

They preached against making calls.
"Kids will get addicted", they said.
"It will call in the cannibals!"
No one listened. The grapevine got
    fed.

That battle had to be fought
So human progress could ring.
There were less cannibals than they
    thought,
But the Shamans were right on one
    thing.

Kids stared at the sky, addicted.
Glassy-eyed, lazy bones.
The same Shamans might have
    predicted
Kids today, staring at their phones.

DINOSAUR FEATHERS

Great Spirit created birds in a breeze
Compared to the dinosaurs.
Birds took to their feathers with ease.
But the dinos acted like lawyers.

Boys were gruff. Their brains were
   itty bitty.
Possibly related to the snake.
They didn't care if they were pretty
If they could make the earth shake.

But female dinos saw the birds
And loved the outfits they were in.
They bandied a few legal words
And moved for feathers on their skin.

They objected to maternity,
And to get live birth reversed
They agreed to lay eggs for eternity

Unless the world ended first.

Lastly, in spite of these gains,
And aware of their limitations
They petitioned for big bird brains
And good marital relations.

That last was nice, so Great Spirit
   waved "Bye!"
He must be many other places.
But girl dinos were just being wry.
They didn't want their own divorce
   cases.

So the boys didn't wear feathers.
Old ones already had a missus,
And usually skins like leather.
But the young ones sure chased the
   misses.

DINO-BIRDS

Now those big feathered dinos are
    gone
With their slippery, bandying words.
But their family lines still live on.
The Dinos have become birds.

So those idle birds at your feeders?
Their grandmas worked hard
    chewing grasses.
Now these modern day succeeders
Just sit on their gluteus masses.

And that works for the raptors.
Who have always been apex
Related in earth's early chapters

To their granddaddy, T-Rex.

Their Agreement with the Great
    Spirit
Still holds. They all lay eggs.
He built them for that, as I hear it.
All egg-layers have bow legs.

P.S. Bats came from ancient fake
    birds.
Like Pterodactyls. They should wear
    wigs.
Putting feathers on those ugly turds
Would be like lipstick on pigs.

SCHOOLS OF FISH

A natural law, earth's symphony,
Is what keeps prey fish in schools.
Unnatural laws make us agree
To obey all government rules.

Unnatural music keeps us in line
Swimming one way, then we turn,
    like fish.
With humans it weakens the spine
Until your vertebrae squish.

Governments, even the remotest,
Emit pacifying melodies.
It's shepherd music. You've never
    noticed.
But they can make you pee your
    undies.

You might do that in Red China
If you don't swim like other fish.
So talk like a parrot, or a mynah!
Eat anything they put in your dish.

Just follow the music! Don't read
    this.
Because fish that fall out of school
Are eaten, every mister or miss.
That's the conductor's Golden Rule.

Or – since the music comes from the
    city –
Go outside. Show them your rear.
Country folk sing their own ditty
We don't get their music out here.

COVID CANNIBALS

Covid was trouble for everyone
But toughest on poor cannibals.
Once the lockdown had begun
It led to some serious brawls.

No tribesman ran away, for fear
Of catching deathly covid out *there*
When they might get lucky *here.*
They drew lots to make this fair.

They had reason to be optimistic.
They got news. They had radio.
It was *lockdown*, home *cooking*. Not
    idealistic.
But only for 2 weeks or so!

But then the radio said
The lockdown had been extended.
They counted up who wasn't dead:
There were 10. All fat ones. Splendid!

Time flies when you're having fun,
But to the last guy's frustration
When he was the only one,
He died of starvation.

The lockdown did lift, after a while,
Like the whole world hoped it would.
But only on this jungle isle
Did it ever do some good.

GOBLIN BATS

When Old World tribes walked the
    bridge
To America on the other side
They found a land as cold as your
    fridge
And caves, already occupied.

No sweat. Cave lions and bears
Could be got rid of with spears.
But there were bats too, millions of
    pairs
And goblins had lived there for years.

Those two go together, did you
    know?
Goblins knew all the bat caves.
Goblins taught them to fly long ago.
They've become little goblin slaves.

Goblins are all alike.

They will gobble your child, so take
    note:
To regurgitate the tyke
Stick your finger down that throat.

But bats are unique, OK?
When clouds of them fly through
Morning and evening, twice a day
The kids saw what bat radar can do.

For excitement every cave kid
Dodged the bat swarm as it came.
Of course that was strictly forbid,
But it's more fun than a video game.

Homeowners of today have flies,
And mosquitoes and gnats,
And swatters, should need arise,
But you should just try to swat bats.

DEODORANT

In this **Age of Deodorant**
Advertising has arranged
To replace **B.O.** with a sweeter scent.
Because of this our climate changed.

B. O. was natural, not just waste.
Its loss will cause abnormalities.
And it hated to be replaced
By products called 'Toiletries'.

B.O. is 98.6 degrees.
You could see it move a windsock.
A million people make quite a
    breeze,

And that breeze moves north around
    the clock.

So the Arctic feels it first.
What to do? Follow climate science!
We can get all of this reversed
With **100%** compliance.

Dump your underarm and aftershave!
Quit washing! All boys at least.
Just think of the **B.O.** we could save!
That's how to tame the climate beast.

BLACK HOLES

Somewhere out there in the cosmos
Black holes are inching together.
Will they attract, or will they oppose?
Astronomy should tell us whether.

Oops. No telescope handy.
But just off the top of my head
There'll be a marriage. A dandy!
Probably in the infrared.

Black Holes are magnets with two
    poles
So it's even money with legal tender

What happens with those Black
    Holes,
But I'm hoping they're opposite
    gender.

I saw a picture of this
Or at least a simulation.
I think we're about to see bliss,
And it better be for the duration.

That's my guess: It's a girl and a boy.
But Black Holes don't abide erosion.
So there better be eternal joy!
Or else it's a huge explosion.

THE WITCHES APPRENTICE.

A real witch? You better expect it.
Witchery is one of the trades.
And this wouldn't be the first outfit
Where the foreman came from
    Hades.

Much the same with her hired help:
She's a hag, a fairly young dame.
A right sinful little whelp
And gambling's her favorite game.

When I won our game of poker
And inquired how she handled her
    debts
She paid me off with an Ogre
For which I still have regrets.

She taught me a controlling spell,
Sort of snickering and gloating,
"Eye of newt, anus of camel – "
Forgive me! I am only quoting.

She rattled off the whole charm,

No use repeating it here.
Left me with an Ogre on my arm,
And proceeded to disappear.

Yikes! We're not allowed to have
    those mutants.
They're mean! Bloodthirsty!
    Barbaric!
They're made of all kinds of
    pollutants.
My wife would go hysteric.

I steered him into the Cloaca,
The sloppy sewer of Rome.
Not exactly a mocha-snacka
But he seemed to like his new home.

That sewer is still used today.
Don't go in there if you love your life.
It has one good use, some will say:
To get rid of a nerve wracking wife.
    ~Cassius Virtuous.

RENDER UNTO PHAROAH

Don't be shocked. Pharoah levied
    taxes.
He had his 'Scribes', his IRS.
The Scribes had whips and axes.
So tax day involved some stress.

At first, when Scribes were new,
They forced Village Chiefs to pay.
But as the Scribe Bureau grew
They nailed everyone, just like today.

What taxes do you have to pay?
Income and sales? Plus a lot more?
Do you fudge a bit in your own way?
It's all been done before.

Some favorites were exempted,
The Priesthood and the Scribe
    Bureau.
Everyone else was tempted

But nobody else paid zero.

"Everyone paid", the Chief Scribe
    wrote
In his report. But it's human nature
To let a few decimals 'float'
Just like our Legislature.

We should touch on Final Expenses.
The Pyramids assured reincarnation.
All free for Pharoah, no
    consequences.
But what about poor people's
    salvation?

A few did save up for caskets.
But you can bet your dinero
Those who went out in garbage
    baskets
Are as well off now as Pharoah.

EV'S VS. CORDLESS TOOLS

"The day will come!" (You've heard
    the theories,
And now they teach it in schools)
…When there won't be enough
    batteries
For both EV's and cordless tools".

They say earth is zero sum.
When resources are gone, they're
    gone.
Let's take that as a rule of thumb
And choose what we need to go on.

Take the electric automobile.
Is it really necessary?
Despite how good it makes you feel
Most people are pretty wary.

What about cordless tools then?
The building trades use them all.

But should there even be tradesmen
When our resources are so small?

Let's list some cons and pros.
EV's are higher status, that's true.
And they save the planet, some
    suppose.
Because they don't fart CO2.

But they're costly, and gasoline cars
Save the planet too – what I mean,
Is all that CO2 of ours
Is what makes this planet green.

So there's a good, cheap alternative
To EV's. What about cordless tools?
Don't grab them from the hardhats
    where I live
Or they'll break your nose, you fools.

Dancing Neanderthals

We know Neanderthals died out
Although some DNA lives on.
But old footprints tell a lot about
The Neanderthal phenomenon.

He was light-footed, a glider, a
    leaper.
These are correct answers,
Or his footprints would have been
    deeper.
Neanderthal was a dancer!

Okay. Now I understand.
Neanderthals did overlap

With Cro-Magnons, a neighboring
    band,
Pretty smoothly, like ASAP.

There probably were parties like ours
And as evening was advancing,
Cro-Magnon boys would be
    wallflowers.
Neanderthal dudes would be
    dancing.

Is dancing the way to a girl's heart?
I dunno. I'm all Cro-Magnon.
So if my girl was there to take part
I might have lost her to an ape-man.

A New Worry

The future should have looked
    splendid
11,700 years ago.
That's when the Ice Age ended,
Give or take a year or so.

But some doubted the weather.
There was fear it might reverse,
Like, do the opposite altogether:
Overheat! That could be worse.

Lots of anecdotes were quoted.
Some oldsters still remembered ice.
In the end the people voted
To phase out fire, to sacrifice.

That was settled in the spring
Following a winter without snow.
They rejoiced, and the wind did
    bring
A warm summer, wouldn't you
    know?

So they reduced the campfires by
    half.

No problem, though their meat was
    now rare.
"Rare is good!" said the Chief with a
    laugh.
And Autumn came with more balmy
    air.

They cut the fires in half again
When winter came way late.
"It'll soon be spring!" laughed the
    brave men
As raw meat bled out on their plate.

They hadn't put up much firewood.
Then blizzards started and didn't
    stop.
The Chief mumbled, "This ain't
    good."
And deep snow drifted over the top.

Other villages had put up wood.
There hadn't been any confusion.
Their DNA lives on, as it should.
Be happy you survived evolution.

Venus

For Zeus, the beautiful sirens
Presented a paradox.
He should have clapped them in
    irons
For luring ships to crash on the
    rocks.

But they were least of the Greek
    Gods
So he banished them to Venus.
They lost their satyr boyfriends, poor
    broads.
Their new boss was ugly Silenus.

The Great Zeus added a parting shot,
"If any earthling sees you, you'll die".
Even then Venus was hot,
But at least there were clouds in that
    sky.

The clouds saved them these many
    years.
They peeked out, but that was all.
They're safe until the weather clears,
But if anyone comes – LOL!

That will happen. Spy rockets!
Ask the Martians. It's been done
    before.
(Your government has deep pockets.)
But the sirens aren't there anymore.

Zeus relented in the nick of time.
He pulled the curse. He's such a
    dear.
He arranged airfare on the taxpayers
    dime
And he brought them all back here.

WISDOM

If Wisdom is the current sum
Of human experience
But some was scrapped, by rule of
    thumb
We now make less than perfect
    sense.

Happily for the human race
We can stretch our minds enough
To reach back through time and
    space
And dredge up the discarded stuff.

Yikes! Some was gory and
    unpleasant.
Leave that for the anoscope.
The rest we'll bring up to the present
Using storyteller soap.

Hmm…this looks like *beastly*
    knowledge.
It must've come from their scrap
    heap.
Well, Beasties never went to college
But their stuff is great! And also
    cheap.

I love their wisdom. It makes me
    grin.
Not so most world leaders. They love
    war.
That only proves which end their
    brain is in.
You're safer with the hungry Beasts
    of Yore.

ZOMBIES

No one ever asks the little guy
But I could make a big score.
Most movies flop. I could tell them
    why.
They're not as much fun anymore.

The new movie stars just stink.
They get millions to bore and irk us.
More kids get this than they think,
Instead they should give us a circus!

They could, and they would make
    money
If they'd only come to their senses.
Zombie stars could be very funny
And also save on expenses.

Say, a few bucks for a backhoe
To dig up enough of 'em
And that's about it, although
Have spray-glue handy. You might
    need some.

Scriptwriters could work cheaper.
If you know Zombies, they mostly
    groan.
I'm not sure about the Grim Reaper
But I'll try to get zombies on loan.

Okay. That part was easy.
But Hollywood doesn't care if it goes
    broke.
They'll just call me dumb and sleazy
Because they love the 'Woke'.

FAIRY RINGS

Fairy lasses loved the stars and sky
And wouldn't give that up for
   romance.
Though each lass had a favorite guy
It never worked out, so they dance.

They dance the Ring when they visit.
They live up in Nyo year-around.
But the 'Ring', if you ask what is it?
It's just their bit of Hallowed ground.

Hallowed to them, not the Almighty.
He thinks all fairies are foolish.
Hopelessly hoity-toity.

And that's true. Fairies are mulish.

But the lasses, after centuries,
Of loneliness, dance the Ring.
On the grass, in the shadow of trees
Hoping lads will come, and they
   sing!

The lads, being underground
Working their mines don't know it.
But hungry trolls do hear this sound,
And they're coming. Hey girls! Don't
   blow it!

SINKHOLES IN THE SKY

Sinkholes on earth can eat cars.
I've seen it. That's a pretty big bite.
But you could escape one of ours.
Not Black Holes. They even eat
    light.

That's tight, but there might be an
    upside.
Galaxies are huge. They spew waste.
If Black Holes flush to the Dark Side
They're cosmic toilets, smartly
    placed.

Or? Are they like an end-of-life trash
    can?

I wouldn't want to take that route.
I hope that's not The Almighty's
    plan.
I think I'd try to climb back out.

Or? Maybe they belong to Satan.
They do say he likes the dark.
If it's The Almighty's light he's hatin'
We could be in big trouble! Hark!

Black Holes lurk out of sight
And suck even galaxies in!
But new stars are born. The
    Heaven's are bright!
I'll take The Almighty to win.

THE GOD/PHARAOHS

All the Great Rulers, historically,
Ran a kingdom or an empire.
But the Pharaohs, at least
    rhetorically.
Climbed a little bit higher.

They declared themselves Gods, by
    criminy.
Of course it wasn't true.
But it sounded good, by jiminy.
So Egyptians worshipped them too.

But that's not what kept people
    content
For several thousand years.
It was festivals! Pharaoh spent
Half his fortune on food, wine, and
    beers.

The Priests even dragged out
Sacred statues of the Pharaoh/Gods
For good luck against flood or
    drought
But in Egypt they had poor odds.

But speaking of the Priesthood,
Pharaoh spent his other half on
    Priests
Who made him look so good
By setting up all the feasts.

A 3rd half went for a pyramid tomb.
Something suitable for a
    God/Pharaoh.
A good-sized one with enough room
For the 4th half: the gold and dinero.

Which still left him with one more
    half
Because when a God/Pharaoh
    couldn't pay
He just raised taxes on the riffraff.
He never raided his IRA.

For millennia Pharaohs were Gods
Though they had human blood and
    marrow.
Can a real God have a human bod?
One did, but He was no Pharaoh.

CAVEMEN AT THE ISTHMUS

Cavemen arrived at the Isthmus
Too soon! There was still open sea.
This happened right at Christmas
Not special yet, but one day it would
    be.

The thought put the Lord in a good
    mood.
Who knew The Almighty's reasons?
With His Chosen Race still in
    prelude
He gave a break to these ones.

The beckoning South American
    shore
Knew not cavemen nor their
    grandkids.

Now it would be peaceful no more,
If these were smart enough
    hominids.

He gave them lumber, hammer and
    nails
To build rafts so they wouldn't get
    wet.
The tools must stay since according
    to tales
They hadn't been invented yet.

That's how South America got settled
Before real civilization.
You might say the Great Spirit
    meddled
But remember, this is His creation.

MAMMOTHS AT THE ISTHMUS

No sooner did the cavemen sally
    forth
And bump ashore on the far side
Than a second group arrived from
    the North
A herd of mammoths stopped, wide-
    eyed.

They also could see the far shore
But there was disagreement between
The 'hims' and the 'hers' they adore
About keeping their hairdos clean.

Girls didn't like the salt water
So they weren't about to swim.
One even asked why her him brought
    her.
The Almighty spoke up on a whim.

He liked the mammoths. They were
    smart.
If He could help them too – why not?

The carpenter stuff, for the most part
Was right there. They could give it a
    shot.

Mammoths quickly grasped the
    mechanics,
And placed boards in a logical
    manner.
But they all felt rising panics
The moment they grasped the
    hammer.

A trunk is a marvelous appendage.
It can do any one thing. Any task.
But only one thing, like a rain gauge.
It can't also hold nails, so don't ask.

They tried teamwork, but here's the
    details:
Every single Miss, or Mrs.
Refused to hold any more nails
After a few of their Mister's misses.

A Man's World

Hey guys! Remember the Good Old
  Days?
It's the man things we mostly recall.
Back when cavemen had vagabond
  ways
The guys really did have it all.

They were hunters and fishermen!
Women drudged, daughters too, but
  not sons.
And if the wives complained back
  then
Their heroes went raiding for new
  ones.

Men ruled the Ice Age while it lasted.
Then a warm wind blew. Very
  strange.

The men watched, flabbergasted,
As the great beasts vanished from
  Climate Change.

The men still hunted and took the
  lead
But the girls made salads for dinner.
When hunting was poor and there
  was need
They became the default
  breadwinner.

And speaking of bread, they raised
  wheat
And ground it into flour.
Thus farming began. Quite a feat.
Who knew there was so much girl
  power?

SEPARATE BATHROOMS

Girl Power brought about the first
    Queen.
Who decreed mankind should settle
    down.
And she ordered a common latrine
When cavemen built the first town.

Being cavemen they used rocks.
The first idea they hit on.
So the low biffy walls were square
    blocks
With an open air log to sit on.

No more 'going behind a tree'.
There would be modern toilet
    hygiene.
The coed part would save money.
Ladies gasped, but she was the
    Queen.

She and her female servants
Lined up on the log to demonstrate.
But then there was a disturbance:
Some guy who just couldn't wait.

Boys have peed off tall mountains,
And written their names in the snow,
And stood proudly to make
    fountains.
They're a hazard wherever they go.

So this guy, perhaps not the smartest,
Just upwind of Her Majesty,
Happened to be a fountain artist,
And the Queen caught the aerosol
    pee.

In a show of common sense
She said that place could go to
    Hades.
And sparing no expense
She built a new one for just ladies.

The new space was safe for every
    dame
Until the 21st century.
And if we had just a Queen to blame
We could fix this with aerosol pee.

MODESTY

Early men were not like the beasts
But you wouldn't know it from their
    looks:
Hairy and naked, the men at least.
But girls dressed – more than they
    show in books.

Cave girls displayed a classy reserve,
A virtue previously unknown.
But their clothes didn't hide every
    curve.
In fact, they made sure some were
    shown.

'Twas modesty the girls had.
Some more, some less, some way
    less.
But beasts don't have it, never had.
It's a trait only humans possess.

So let's give the girls their due.
They started civilization.
They dragged the guys with them
    too,
And clothing became a sensation.

What's that? You want some
    evidence?
There's none. Pretty clothes don't
    fossilize.
But just use your common sense.
Temptation is what lured the guys.

Girls know how to evoke mystery.
And cave girls wore clothes with flair.
Skirts have wiggled throughout
    history.
All the guys can do is stop and stare.

UFO's

Do you believe in UFO's?
Some respectable people do.
They can't all be Pinocchio's
So maybe flying saucers are true.

Will that be our ultimate fate?
To be conquered by little green
    beings?
Or is that just smartphone clickbait?
What *is* it that people are seeing?

Inexplicable lights. Things that
    zoom.
It borders on goofy, forsooth.
They would toss it from any
    courtroom.
But I'm starting to think it's the
    truth,

But first, with the little green men.

I want some solid evidence.
Show us a little green body then!
That's only good common sense.

Since there are no green bodies today
We'll post bounty – a huge reward!
And true to the American way,
It'll be more than we can afford.

We'll set the bag limit at five.
It'll be like the Wild West untamed!
They can bring 'em in dead or alive!
But the bounty may never be
    claimed.

If aliens want to conquer earth
America would give them pause.
We'd be way more trouble than it's
    worth
With our firearm-friendly laws.

THE DRAGON'S BATHROOM

As beastly as male dragons are
They do respect the Ladies Room.
Only one male ever went so far
As to crash their private bathroom.

Ladies lounged there in a sandy cove
Around a bubbling warm pool
Well-hidden by the mangrove,
And he marched right in like a fool.

"Don't worry", he laughed. "Today
    I'm a girl!"
Which hinted at some sort of
    troubles.
And he proceeded to give it a whirl.

He peed way out into the bubbles.

The ladies were totally aghast.
They exploded in virtuous oaths
And they gave him a fiery blast –
You know where, since he had on no
    clothes.

'Twas a surgical strike, you might
    say.
Didn't leave him legless or armless.
Happened just once, back in the day.
The dude had to be rendered
    harmless.

BEASTLY VIRTUES

There's some virtue in every beast.
Not counting the devil's own.
Dormant, maybe. But it's there at
    least.
Some good they may never have
    known.

All the meat eaters come to mind.
They keep the natural balance we
    need.
They don't do it to be kind,
But it amounts to a good deed.

There's not much else they can
    bring.
But dragons, for what it's worth,
Did more than that balancing thing.

They brought nuclear power to earth.

Through the Ages humans have
    wondered
But no human dared to inquire
As the beasts blasted and thundered
What was the source of their fire?

Why, their belly is a living reactor!
They consume uranium ore.
Our geniuses 'borrowed' that factor
And now it's our best tool for war.

The dragons should be jealous.
Their thunder was simply stolen.
But as any witness could tell us
They do love a big explosion.

VOODOO

There's a village known only to
    explorers
That I heard of in barroom chit-chat
Who've never known war or its
    horrors,
Thanks to Voodoo, and an old
    dingbat.

The explorers are coy about this.
They just speak of exotic plants.
Not that village, just tropical bliss.
But I heard they all peed their pants.

The neighboring tribes who are
    warlike
Eye that village with evil intents.
But there's a woman there who
    would like
To give them incontinence.

I may run for President.

I'll hire that dingbat, spare no
    expense.
If I can only win her consent
She'll be my Secretary of Defense.

We could delete the Defense budget.
Thus our deficit will flatten.
She'll cost $24, as I judge it.
Don't laugh. That once bought
    Manhattan.

She'll set up safe perimeters,
Including all Alaskan soil.
Hawaii won't be in the parameters
But so what? They don't have any oil.

We'll be set. No foreign aggressor
Can supply enough fanny wipers
To challenge our dingbat, God bless
    her!
There just ain't enough adult diapers.

RINGS OF SATURN

This is earth's perfect occasion.
Humanity should never have to
    leave.
Our timing works for creation
Or evolution, as some believe.

Either way here we are this fine day!
The weather's good as far as we see.
It's better than Saturn's anyway.
I'm sure Saturnians would agree.

They had real bodies once, like our
    own.
But as the planet got colder
They cast off the bodies they had
    known.
To survive they had to be bolder.

They stretched themselves thinner
    and wider
To catch more of the distant sun
And drifted off Saturn, outside her,
Into orbit. That's how it was done.

Gravity holds them helpless in rings.
The colored rings are for ethnic
    groups.
I write this so you avoid these things.
Don't end up like those dupes.

One day this could happen on earth!
So put on a few pounds! Start today.
You'll be safe with a much bigger
    girth.
It's the skinnies who'll drift away.

ALL-AMERICAN HYGIENE

If not for that fortunate land bridge
When the Ice Age was full blown,
And the brave folks who dared that
    narrow ridge,
Toilet hygiene might still be
    unknown.

They had populated this hemisphere
When Columbus made his big find,
And they've argued ever since that
    year
Which hemisphere did most for
    mankind.

The answer is surprisingly easy.
Everyone has to go #2.
But some of the cleanup was sleazy.
Let's do an in-depth review.

Before toilet paper was invented
Potty odor followed the masses.

In the Old World, no one was sweet-
    scented.
That hemisphere had sore (rhymes
    with gasses).

In the New World they had corn.
A food staple, if a bit spice-less.
They ate lots, even the low-born,
Because leftover cobs were priceless.

So the West had comfier fannies.
Americans never spread dirty vapor.
'Cause they polished up those
    crannies
Using corn cobs for toilet paper.

Some cobs secretly came to Europe
And the Royals began to smell
    sweeter.
Their chronic soreness did clear up.
But no one became a sweet corn
    eater.

CUISINE OF URANUS

So what is the world's best buffet?
Galaxy-wide, the most famous?
At one time everyone would say,
"It's the sausages of Uranus!"

In its geothermal zones
There were small mud pot volcanoes,
Bubbling hot little cones
From which steaming sausages
	arose.

'Tweren't meat nor any vegetable
But a soft and succulent granite.
It was irresistibly edible
Just courtesy of the planet.

Publicity was soon streaming.
A pretty alien could be your guide.
Ah! The smell of those sausages
	steaming!

It drew tourists from far and wide.

Animal Rights groups were first to
	say
That the sausages were alive,
And this was their only way
To escape from there and survive.

That slowed tourism to a stop.
Tourists felt like they had swallowed
	mice.
They all flew home and made their
	drop.
And to be sure, they flushed twice.

That's how we got our unspoken
	rule:
Ask away about cooking and baking
But don't ask, like a silly fool,
What goes into sausage making.

Yoo Hoo's Vision

They say the Ice Age was for men
With barely room for a woman's
    touch.
Caveman school was for boys back
    then.
The girls weren't supposed to learn
    much.

When Yoo Hoo was born into that
    Age
Speech was just grunts, according to
    lore.
But in a dream when she was teenage
She saw an alphabet and wanted
    more!

All in that instant she knew
Every sound that she spoke had a
    letter.

This brainstorm came out of the
    blue.
It made sense, which was even
    better.

26 letters danced in her mind
And attached to the human sounds,
All the spoken sounds of mankind.
A book that big would weigh 10
    pounds.

Now she could teach. But cavemen
    were proud!
How could she deal with mulish
    cavemen?
Grown-ups were a very tough crowd.
So she's thinking. You'll meet Yoo
    Hoo again.

TRADER RATS

Great Spirit gave us the common rat.
The Great Spirit knows best, I
    suppose.
But then, as if to make up for that,
He made Trader Rats. I do like
    those.

Eemert, and Fleamert his brother,
Demanded woolly tails, like sheep.
But then Eemert laughed at the
    other,
Saying, "Fleamert, you look *cheap*".

Great Spirit put them on pause,
Ordered them to be janitor rats,
And made fewer of them because,
By the signs they were borderline
    brats.

They were meant to clean up what
    was messed
By their dirty, common kinfolk.
They did come, they saw, but they
    digressed
As their greedier instincts awoke.

It struck them as justifiable
To 'recover' a valuable trinket
For profit, without being liable
Or prompting the Boss to re-think it.

As the Age of Trader Rats boomed
Eemert ran a big store with
    merchandise.
Eemert himself, now well-groomed
Had a no-haggle asking price.

He could've had a monopoly
But Fleamert undersold him by far.
So when Eemert treated folks
    sloppily
He lost their business. Au Revoir!

Thus Free Market forces were
    revered
In most parts of the earth
So by the time humans appeared
Everyone knew what things were
    worth.

BOUNTY ON DRAGONS

In the dimmest days of the Dark
    Ages
Before King Arthur appeared,
When the Round Table knights were
    just pages,
Dragons ravaged England and were
    feared.

The current King was no fool. He
    knew
Heroes were made, not born.
He offered a bounty to anyone who
Could slay one and bring in its horn.

'Dead or Alive' was no mystery.
That's how they tagged criminals
    who fled.
But for the worst beasts in history,
Such as dragons, they had to be
    dead.

He doubled the reward

Until brave young men couldn't
    resist
And they seized a lance or a sword.
But they perished. They will all be
    missed.

But the King, still no fool, cut a deal,
A treaty with the dragon boss.
It was somewhat less than ideal.
He forked protection money across.

But the Dragon boss, also no fool,
Spurned all the King's offers
(A sure-fire haggling rule)
Until he cleaned out the King's
    coffers.

But as we said, the King was no fool.
He raised taxes, the usual thing.
That's a valuable Royal tool.
It's good to be a King.

CARRYING THE TORCH

Way back in Ice Age antiquity
Men ruled and got all the glory.
American girls hated that iniquity,
Here's a true Ice Age story.

Those Siberian winters were dire.
If your fire went out it was a
    bummer.
Some hero must find new fire
Or no one would live to see summer.

There was a Shaman once, and a
    Chief.
The old Chief was a chauvinist snob.
The other was a pious thief.
Together they chose Oog for that job.

Cannibals did live nearby.
But cannibals aren't very nice.

They'll deal if you want to buy
But Oog worried about the price.

So this hero trudged on and froze
Till Neanderthals gave him hot coals.
That saved his fingers if not his toes
But his thoughts were of home.
    Those poor souls!

Oog was gone but a couple weeks
And returned to their grateful
    applause.
Wait…no one even had cold cheeks!
They had fires aplenty because:

The ladies had traded the old Chief
To the cannibals on a hunch,
For fire, and they threw in the thief
So everyone had a hot lunch.

'BUMP STOCK' ATLATLS

There were terrorists in the Stone
    Age.
One tribal Chief worried a lot.
Atlatls – spear throwers – were the
    new rage.
But they might aim for *him*, might
    they not?

Hunters loved throwers from the first
    day.
The best new technology in years!
They kept the cannibals away.
But the Chief called them 'Bump
    Stock' spears.

One night he declared them
    outlawed.
And confiscated them all at dawn.
Or I should say, he sent his goon
    squad
But the rest of the tribe was gone.

Probably a 'birdie' had been
    chirping.
Anyhow, cannibals paid a visit.
There were sounds like slurping and
    burping.
That's not too ghoulish, is it?

In a few weeks the tribe returned.
Their huts still stood. They didn't
    lose them.
But the Chief and his goons had
    'adjourned'.
I won't lie, that part amused them.

The Chief and his squad, the dirty
    cops
Were reduced to bones too big for
    pots.
But the cannibals were good moms
    and pops.
They took the wishbones home for
    their tots.

THEY SHALL RETURN

The best way to rate civilization
If you want an accurate gauge
Is the housing of the population
Starting back in the Stone Age.

Caves were free back then, but
    beware
You don't want beasts living there
    too.
So the cost would be killing the bear
Before the cave bear killed you.

In time, when the caves were all filled
And the tribes scattered helter-skelter
They learned huts were easy to build
Wood was free and made decent
    shelter.

When farms and villages appeared
Money had been invented.
But homes were cheap if the land
    wasn't cleared.
All families had them. No one rented.

Then, big homes. Big debt. Big
    monthly bills.
The rat race kicked up with inflation.
Mansions sprang up in the hills.
That marked the high point of our
    nation.

High prices and cost of living
Blocked our way. Not to be
    judgmental,
But unaffordable is unforgiving.
So lots of us found a rental.

It won't stop there. It'll go viral.
Just watch. There'll be vagrant
    hordes.
You can't stop that downward spiral.
Homelessness is what we're heading
    towards.

But praise to Old Mother Earth!
Caves are empty again. They're
    beckoning.
We'll start over, for what it's worth.
This isn't our first day of reckoning.

DIET APPS

So many American guys
And be honest, a few new Mamas,
Notice their bellies, or butts or thighs
Should be covered with pajamas.

We know! We all know we should
   diet
And drop a few pounds here or there.
Most of us don't want to try it,
But that's not because we don't care.

For all these people here's some good
   news.
There's an app for this or soon will
   be.
You can eat anything you choose.
It's expensive, but the food is free.

First there'll be a consultation.
Nurse will check your available
   credit.
You can do this at her workstation.

Just sign, whether or not you've read
   it.

Your receptor will be implanted,
Probably in your belly button.
After that you can take for granted
There's no harm in being a glutton.

Now find the snacks at your
   shopping center.
Scan the bar code of any yummy,
And click your belly button to 'enter'.
This will give you a happy tummy.

Someday there'll be options for
Receptors on your taste buds too,
And probably in your back door
To confirm it all passed through.

All this will soon be just clicks away!
Until then you could cut back.
Just eat a little less each day
And get your shapely butt back.

THE REAL WONDER

The Seven Ancient Wonders
Are like strippers who don't twerk.
I rate them all as blunders.
None of them ever did any work.

It didn't matter, old or newer,
They just sat there. The pyramids
    still sit.
Kings built them instead of a sewer.
So their cities stank from *it.*

It was Romans who built the great
    Cloaca,
That sewer drained all of Rome with
    ease.
It turned the Tiber into *Cloaca*
    Mocha,
When it flushed the Temple of
    Hercules.

That Temple, in the old days of
    Rome,
Was the daily toilet of their gods.
That's what happens with a mortal
    genome.
All their gods had physical bods.

The Cloaca walls take a beating
When a Roman god volleys and
    thunders.
It's worse when a bunch are
    competing.
That sewer should be one of the
    wonders.

For sure it should go number 2
It might even go number 1.
If anything beats the pyramid of
    Khufu,
It's a bowel movement, well done.

DAYCARE

The cavemen had a good hunt!
So for the next several days
The ladies would be out front
Doing butchering, as always.

It was a great day for a Paleo tribe
When good days for cavemen were
    rare
But Yoo Hoo, the young would-be
    scribe,
Was always stuck doing daycare.

Just a word about the caveman child,
They were much like beasts if you
    please.
Both were equally wild
And most of them had fleas.

They spoke in grunts like a beast
And the parents weren't much better.
Yoo Hoo vowed that she would at
    least
Introduce the brats to a letter.

She fancied herself as their teacher
But one girl was already astray

Up a tree where no one could reach
    her.
That's where Yoo Hoo carved the
    letter 'A'.

The others fetched pieces of wood
And scratched 'A's on them with an
    arrow.
Yoo Hoo smiled. They were doing so
    good!
But their attention span was narrow.

As dusk fell, "Pick up and do
    chores!"
Shouted the village crier.
Yoo Hoo was about to give them
    scores
When they tossed the schoolwork
    into the fire.

The letter 'A' was gone, you might
    say,
Before she could even announce it.
But keep an eye on Yoo Hoo; one
    day
She'll invent a way to pronounce it.

ROAD-KILL ALIENS

Aliens have been here. They're here
    now.
The way I heard it, they're stranded.
Saucer ran out of fuel somehow.
They had no choice, so they landed.

That was thousands of years ago
And now we call them raccoons.
Trouble for our world but even so,
They do have cute wiggly moons.

Every year there's a new brood.
We just shot 'em when I was a kid.
They're very rude. Want to know how
    rude?

They will poop on your toilet lid.

But just when you think they're
    piggish
You notice they wash all their food.
They're fastidious, even priggish,
And that softens your mood.

But they don't understand road
    traffic.
If only they were good on the grill!
I wish this wasn't so graphic,
But they are the most common road
    kill.

ICE AGE WEATHERMEN

They had weather in the Ice Age.
Below the glaciers they got summer.
A weatherman invented the rain
    gauge.
Cavemen weren't all dumb and
    dumber.

That guy with the gauge was a seer.
A weather Seer, ridiculed a lot.
But his forecasts portended fear
So the scorn kept out of earshot.

Aside from the Shaman and Chief
The Seer made the best living.
But unlike them he wasn't a thief.
He earned it through almsgiving.

He would only accept a small fee
So rich folk asked just for fun.
The poorest folk got it for free,
But they never got a good one.

He made sure to leave someone
    crabby
So they would buy a private forecast.

That was his scam. Not too shabby!
And it was always better than the
    last.

So he was sure of a handsome fee.
But when that forecast hit the
    grapevine
He wasn't accorded so handsomely.
They all thought, "His is better than
    mine!"

Bear in mind though, he was pretty
    good.
And a forecast was welcome each
    day.
It's only fair that the whole tribe
    should
Reward him with excellent pay.

We still ridicule and doubt 'em
But they're paid well now, no need to
    scam.
They're on TV. We shouldn't laugh
    about 'em.
It's the weather itself that's flim-flam.

SMILODON'S BIRTHDAY

Would you like a cuddly Smilodon?
Let's hope they don't clone them for
    pet stores.
Of all the old beasts that are bygone
He's the worst that walked on all
    fours.

They've found a good sabretooth
    fang
And scraped off some good DNA.
So they do have both yin or yang
And they're ready to clone right
    away.

They need a neutral, surrogate Mom
Big enough for the job, I guess.
They searched with no visible qualm
And chose a cute lioness.

Following this rare cloning
They'll settle on an Ice Age birthdate,
And the question of who is owning,
And should they clone him a mate?

Using radiocarbon dating
They pegged Smiley as an April
    baby.
Of which year? They're still debating.
Could be 15,000 BC – maybe.

They had expected an August date.
Because they're reserved for Leos,
    dummy.
But maybe his Mom can't wait.
Oh well, now he'll have a new
    Mummy.

We'll still try to get that August date
    right!
Tricky birth tho – with long teeth like
    a saber.
It's April. Four months to go. Sit
    tight!
Oops! She's going into labor.

And here comes Old Smiley, paws
    first.
Wait a sec. That's not claws, it's
    hooves.
The cloning team watches, fearing
    the worst,
Still hoping the baby improves.

But it turns out to be a calf.
We flip him over, he's the same
    underneath.
So that's Smiley's epitaph:
He's dead, except what's stuck on his
    teeth.

THE TOWER OF BABBLE

There was a king, probably Nimrod,
Who pondered a tower back when,
That would reach all the way up to
    God.
For that job he needed lots of good
    men.

He hired everyone for the duration,
Simply because he can,
To build this pride of his nation,
And now he had enough good men.

They built seven stories each year,
Working overtime now and then.
Every night they drank tankards of
    beer
Because they were good and thirsty
    men.

Nimrod, who would be God, was still
    young

When the tower reached the clouds,
    and then,
The workers prayed and hymns were
    sung
Because they really were good men.

Then God bestowed strange tongues
    to each.
Nimrod's orders made no sense then.
Confusion reigned. It was Freedom
    of Speech
That stopped that tower. Amen.

They all went off on their own, that
    crew,
And ever since that's how it's been.
There's no secret, as your boss could
    tell you,
It's just tough to keep good men.

THE DRY SAHARA

Do you worry about earth's orbit?
Or how it wobbles through space?
Well, it has a rhythm like your butt
Except it wiggles at a much slower
    pace.

Earth wobbled five thousand years
    ago,
Give or take, and Africa changed.
The dry Sahara began to grow.
The dust storm cycle is pre-arranged.

North Africa would become desert.
That's not fair. It was populated.
Deserts don't care. They're dust and
    dirt.
So gradually they all migrated.

Some went in all directions
Homeless now in the sun's hot glare.
Most went to Egypt despite
    objections
Of the mighty civilization there.

A howl went up from the citizens
About the dirty wilderness tribes.

And at first they managed to cleanse
The bums from Egypt, so say the
    scribes.

Then Pharoah got a brainstorm.
If it's the last thing he ever did
He would welcome the uncouth
    swarm
And they would build him a pyramid!

The migrants gladly worked for
    cheap.
But those blocks! Man, the work was
    sweaty.
Yet they daren't say "dang" or
    ("bleep"),
Or Pharoah might bring in some
    Yeti.

This became competitive, of course.
Each Pharoah/God had a bigger
    ego.
And they had such a cheap work
    force.
So we got the Great Pyramids,
    Amigo!

Lucy

Lucy hit the news like a bombshell.
Or *Celebrity*, if that is preferred.
This 3 million year old human belle
Had been dug up by some nerd.

This proved the evolution theory
And set the morning news a-buzzin'.
I have doubts about this, Dearie.
But they're sayin' she's everyone's
    cousin.

Are we really related to Miss Lucy?
3 million years later I'm not sure.
She walked on two feet, possibly.
But this is all way premature.

For a hominid to be human
They must *think* like humans do.
They need logic and acumen.
Most girls have modesty too.

I wish I could've heard her talking.

Her speech probably needed
    improvements.
And I would love to see her walking!
Human girls have attractive
    movements.

The condition of her bones
Shows she wasn't anyone's feast.
So even before cellphones
She was smarter than the average
    beast.

I begin to admire Miss Lucy.
If she was actually a nice 'Miss',
And not just some kind of floozy,
She might have been fun to kiss.

Whoa! I saw a picture of Lucy.
There'll be no kissin'! I won't do it.
Doctor Leaky, I don't see what you
    see.
You just took your Grant Money and
    blew it.

SNOWBALL EARTH

It happened one fateful day or night
Many, many years ago.
The Great Spirit thought the time
    was right
To populate earth, but it was all
    snow.

He chose earth anyway, back then.
To be home one day for His Chosen
    Ones.
But a snowball was no place for men.
No place for His daughters and sons.

He stoked the fire and warmed the
    sun

So a comfier wind would blow.
Now our thermostats get that job
    done.
We were born in His image, you
    know.

We haven't lived up to that though.
Social tipping points are tipping,
As anyone can see, it's not slow.
Civilization is slipping.

Depravity, crime and war abound.
If He gives up on us, baby,
He'll turn the thermostat back down,
Snow us under and start over.
Maybe.

ENGLISH ACCENT

Was there such a tribe as the
  English?
A pure race with its own DNA?
No. They were very commingle-ish.
Just a mixed bag, you might say.

The British Isles and Ireland too
Were once covered 2 miles deep
With ice, as you probably knew.
There was no life then. Not a peep.

Then earth wobbled. The climate
  reversed.
A small English channel was waded.
The French and the Dutch came
  first.
After that the Vikings invaded.

We won't count Neanderthals, of
  course,
Who came and went with Ice Ages.
But many tribes came. Some came in
  force.
England's story has violent pages.

But after a few millenniums,
They came together, Buttercup.
And in just a few bienniums

The English language bubbled up.

What finally made that doable
Was an accent that can't be
  deciphered.
All agreed English was pursuable
So long as no one understood one
  word.

Is that any way to run a great nation
Where nobody knows what they've
  heard?
There'd be so much frustration!
But someone does have the last
  word.

The Royal Stenographer at Court!
All the rulings are in her hand.
From Great Treaties to child support.
By herself she saves Merry Old
  England.

She decides what the witnesses
  meant.
The Stenographer writes the law.
But what causes that British accent?
It's the nose pulling up on the jaw.

THE GREAT EXTINCTIONS

We lost them! Every last Ice Age
    beast.
Mainly because cavemen killed 'em.
I think they used every part, at least.
Mainly because they grilled 'em.

Some will say it was climate change.
That beasts died when the Ice
    unfroze.
But ice came and went, so that's
    strange.
The beasts lived through several of
    those.

They say other factors were at work.
That humans played a smaller part.
That the weather just went berserk
Because cavemen weren't all that
    smart.

I won't judge anyone's ancestors.
There's too much rioting anyway.
I don't say this to attract protesters.
But cavemen were genius for their
    day.

They were smarter than the great
    beasts.
They made spears and spear
    throwers.
I wish I could've been at their feasts
And hung out with their partygoers.

Yup, that's what caused the
    extinctions:
The human mind and what it can do.
If you won't give us that distinction
That's dumb, and I guess you are
    too.

BALANCING THE DIET

The human race has always been
    gassy.
And it's mostly the boys who are
    rude.
They laugh when it's really brassy.
But the girls look for healthier food.

They knew instinctively it was diet
They searched for good berries and
    dug roots.
But nothing seemed to make the
    boys quiet.
Truth was, they just liked to make
    toots.

Scholars also have an explanation
Why hunting failed and farming took
    hold.

But it was ladies seeking aeration
Through healthier food, truth be told.

They didn't count calories then
But nutrition was on their mind.
Veggie meals weren't popular with
    men.
But they helped with that gas down
    behind.

Now, with a modern, balanced diet
Boys smell better than in the past.
But there's some who can still start a
    riot
With an old-fashioned cave-clearing
    blast.

CHILLBANES

Old trappers of the far North
Where the Ice Age still remains
Are aware when they venture forth
They're at the mercy of the
    chillbanes.

The 'Banes heed the Queen of that
    land.
They're the gale in her blizzard.
They live only for her command.
That's not good. She's a bad wizard.

This wizard, I should say their
    Queen,
Watches time in its longer stages.
She lets the chillbanes play in-
    between
The Great Epochal Ice Ages.

When the earth wobbles the wrong
    way
Every hundred thousand years or so
It lengthens our winters of today
Into centuries, so glaciers grow.

That will be the prime of the
    chillbanes
And their Queen's greatest might.
We should stop this if we have any
    brains.
Ice Ages are awful, and chillbanes
    bite!

Thankfully, we're on the right track.
We can stop those glaciers from
    forming,
And maybe melt the current ones
    back
If we work hard at Global Warming!

METHIONINE

Decent homes are a modern creation.
Dry and warm and (mostly) clean.
Importantly, there is modern
    ventilation
To get rid of methionine.

There's always some guy, some
    callous beggar
Who, in spite of fans, et cetera,
Will blast out a rotten egger.
Girls don't do this. I asked my Ma.

But let's imagine back in the Ice Age.
A small cave, a family's home.
Some guy's gas and sphincter engage
And now you can read this in a
    poem!

But it gets worse, it always does.
He's a typical caveman.
He's been eating fatty meat because
Mammoths are fatty, so he can!

Thus, kids learn to run at a young
    age.
Mom and brats must run from the
    creep.
They watch for Pop's pressure gauge:
He lifts his leg in his sleep.

So is this why the Paleo tribes
Quit the caves to live outside?
"It's likely", say the better scribes.
"How would you like to be a new
    bride?"

THE TAJ MAHAL

The Taj Mahal was built for Mumtaz,
The Ruler's wife, whom he held
    sublime.
We'll talk more about her because
His name is harder to rhyme.

We will give him credit that's due
For an architectural wonder
But the pyramids are bigger. That's
    true.
And this thing was likely a blunder.

The Taj Mahal didn't come cheap.
According to modern scholars
The cost – not including upkeep –
Was eighty million dollars.

That was a lot of dough back then.

So other needs were neglected.
But what Rulers want to do, they can.
In those days they weren't elected.

Mumtaz must have been pure of
    heart
To be held in such high esteem,
Loved throughout the Realm, a
    sweetheart.
But the Taj Mahal wasn't her dream.

I don't think Mumtaz would've built
    it.
I think she was more like my wife.
The money would've gone where she
    saw fit
To give the people a better life.

Angkor Wat

What mystery pervades Angkor Wat,
One of history's greatest has-beens?
The answer's easier than I thought.
It's all about Siamese twins.

It was part of the Khmer Empire!
Angkor Wat was the crown jewel.
The mighty ruins still inspire.
Then came conjoined Royal Twins!
   Not cool.

Joined at the butt, facing away,
The boys barely acknowledged each
   other
Although they had the same birthday
And the same loving mother.

What a predicament it would be.
The boys were in line to be kings.
But there can't be two kings, you see.
There's no fudging some of these
   things.

It gets worse. One was a Democrat,
The other a Republican.
There's no elections in Angkor Wat,
So when the old King died, what's
   the plan?

Just tell the truth? No way, sunshine!

Civil war would likely ensue.
The people would see it as a sign
That the Empire should split in two.

So they fashioned a gilded portal
Where each day one kid could strut.
And the people could see he was
   mortal
But they couldn't see the bro' on his
   butt.

Luckily, the Royal Lads agreed!
Maybe the first time ever.
And they really did this deed.
But it didn't last forever.

The Democrat twin ordered one
   thing.
The next day his brother reversed it.
It drove folks away, this wild swing.
They abandoned Angkor Wat and
   quit.

That ended two-party politics.
So the world was ruled by pompous
   kings
Until America's democratic fix.
But now we're getting the same wild
   swings.

CHOSEN ONES?

Great Spirit begot His Chosen Ones.
In the Bible that's what we're taught.
But with all today's daughters and
    sons
I wonder who is – and who's not?

The Bible does offer one clue.
It describes beards on all the old
    guys.
Does that description fit you?
Are you Chosen, like that implies?

Of course that would leave out the
    cavemen.
In all the pictures I've seen.
So it leaves out some very brave men.
Just because of a stupid gene.

They populated this hemisphere.
That should win some respect at
    least.

Other beardless races, from what I
    hear,
Populated the Far East.

No beards! So they can't be Chosen
    Ones.
But the rest of the world qualifies.
Including all the Holy Land's sons,
All the Muslim and African guys.

Let's settle this mano-a-mano.
Like we did when the lands were
    frozen.
Fight it out like Rocky Marciano!
Whoever wins is The Chosen.

Let some guy with a beard, some
    tough dude
Walk into, let's say the Sioux Nation
And brag he's Chosen, but they're
    screwed.
I'd pay to see that confrontation.

THE LETTER "B"

You may remember young Yoo Hoo.
Her Daycare nudged kids away
From the caveman grunts they were
    used to
By teaching them the letter "A".

It launched their formal education.
Cave kids had none of that prior.
But that lesson died by cremation.
The kids tossed it into the fire.

That's a lousy start for daycare
    school.
That lesson flopped. No use denying.
But with kids there's a Golden Rule,
If they're awful you just keep trying.

So when she had them after dark
'Round a fire, somewhat attentively,
She gave them all scraps of birch
    bark

And taught them to make the letter
    "B".

She said "B" was for the Boogeyman
Who lurked beyond the firelight.
He was part of her new lesson plan:
An ogre who grabs kids at night!

She added ghosts and blood and
    more
To make them remember the letter,
But as she described the guts and
    gore
A girl laughed. It didn't upset her.

She said saber tooths were tougher.
Cave kids! You just gotta admire.
But their education did suffer.
When they tossed the birch bark into
    the fire.

DUST OF AFRICA

Every 20,000 years, you should know,
The Sahara turns wet and green
For just 10,000 years or so,
And it's terribly dry in-between.

But Mother Nature used the dry
    years
To blow Sahara dust storms west,
To vaccinate a new Hemisphere.
Just the plants, though. She felt that
    was best.

So wherever the dust might touch
The greenery was exposed
To new pathogens, but not much.
One day that would help, she
    supposed.

Now that day was looming.

Columbus had arrived from Spain.
And the New World plants did keep
    blooming!
But the humans would feel some
    pain.

The Spaniards and the New Worlders
Would trade some nasty germs.
And there'd be war for hundreds of
    years
Before everyone came to terms.

Through it all there was beautiful
    scenery.
All the bad was balanced by that
    plus.
Mother Nature saved all the
    greenery.
Not her job to make sense of us.

FAMILY TREE ROYALTY

Have you ever traced your ancestry?
Do you think you have Royal
    relations?
It's a likely sign of Royalty
If you trace lots of generations.

They were the pride of every
    Monarch.
Validation for their vanities.
20 was the usual benchmark
In the better Royal Families.

History is full of Royal news
Their feuds, their affairs, their wars.
Some wars served mostly to amuse
And make a King look good in
    memoirs.

So the Royals did very well.
For thousands of years they lived
    their joke.
But like the Brits say, "What the 'ell!

What's in it for the average bloke?"

Not much. The routine didn't vary.
The serfs received mostly zeroes.
Blokes die in wars; widows re-marry.
They must raise a new crop of
    heroes!

My own family tree is short, and,
I don't see any Royalty at all.
A cow herder and a one-armed
    coachman
They're my guys. To me they stand
    tall.

We wasted centuries with Royal
    Duds,
Kings and Queens and all the rest.
So if you're searching for Royal
    Blood,
Less is better and none is best.

THE DIRT

Modern civilization began
When cavemen learned what dirt
    could do.
It unlocked a future no ape-man
Would think of or aspire to.

Cave girls viewed it with elation.
They turned spear points into garden
    hoes!
Okay, that's exaggeration
But it's the lifestyle they would've
    chose.

Gardens led to villages and homes.
Men, the great hunters and charmers
Who now worked with clays and
    loams
Were still hunters, but now also
    farmers.

The fruit of the dirt, you might say,
Soon supported some big empires
Which had big populations, by the
    way,
And fat Royals, which an empire
    requires.

That's when human progress took a
    pause.
If peasants raised extra to sell
It didn't help, so they didn't, because
The extra went for taxes as well.

Nothing changed for thousands of
    years.
There was little hope for the masses.
Then a new world – America! –
    appears
No kings and Queens or social
    classes!

Land was cheap, if you could get
    there.
And many a poor land-bound serf
Unbound themselves and scraped up
    fare
For a chance to own their own turf.

They became our sodbuster pioneers.
Their lives were dirtier than yours.
Life was tough but there weren't
    many tears.
That was before Tax Auditors.

They wrested a living from the dirt
With their heroic wives and 12 kids
Who somehow grew up unhurt
From the lack of an electric grid.

But sodbusters don't live forever.
Then the same preachers who marry
    'em
Perform one last endeavor.
They plant 'em in the dirt and bury
    'em.

EARTH'S TWIN PLANET

The notion is a bit eerie
But it could be legit.
There are two earths, in theory,
They're equal but opposite.

Astronomers would be unaware
With the bright sun right between us.
Both planets would have the same air
And the same rowdy kids on a school
    bus.

Perhaps, for what it's worth,
We aren't meant to know
That we're also on that other earth.
Another of us. Our alter-ego.

We would be opposite in age
So when we croak, our younger
    double
Will be just barely teenage

And ready to get into trouble.

With luck we'll see, from the Other
    Side
And whisper some advice in advance.
We should. We were just as wild-
    eyed,
And we'll give ourselves a second
    chance.

Of course you may have this figured
    wrong.
You shouldn't assume at a glance
That we are playing *your* swan song.
You might be *their* second chance.

If you are the second chance
You might check out Christianity.
You can still hitch up your pants
And do something for humanity.

THE COMPANY STORE

It started with English factories
Paying out wages "in kind".
And it led to some wretched stories
When legal slavery was just fine.

When it spread to the colonies
American mining companies
Used tokens to put the squeeze
On their workers, with no apologies.

Payday did seem more real this way.
Just like money! Who could ask for
  more?

But it was, on any given day,
Only good at the Company Store.

So they never saved up and moved
For generations this was done.
Their lives only improved
When the union battle was won.

Never again, right? Never again!
Be independent! Don't forget!
But just two generations from then
We repeat it with credit card debt.

THE DENTIST

There's no dragon dentists anymore.
Their insurance doesn't cover fire.
So if a tooth hurts too much to ignore
And must be pulled – who could they
    hire?

No one in their right mind will do it.
But Santa could address this need.
The dragon Blacktooth Jack knew it
And asked for Rudolf to do this deed.

Rudolf knew he shouldn't.
He warned Old Jack about fire.
And Jack promised that he wouldn't.
So we'll see. Jack was known as a liar.

They harnessed the Red-Nosed
    Reindeer

With a long, stout rope to the tooth
And a crowd of elves gathered to
    cheer
And it worked! It came out, forsooth!

But it hurt and Jack blasted flames.
They burned the hair off Rudolf's
    butt.
There were gasps. I won't name
    names
But one reindeer said, "I'll tell you
    what…

That hair better all grow back.
If it doesn't you'd better believe
Rudolf won't be leading the pack.
We won't follow *that* on Christmas
    Eve!"

THE LETTER "C"

It's true that feisty Miss Yoo Hoo,
Too young to be a real schoolmarm,
Got nowhere with letters one and
    two.
But could the letter "C" be the
    charm?

They've got a kitty, her kids do.
A darling, orphaned sabretooth.
Orders are: "Take it back". Oh, boo-
    hoo!
The kitty loved them, forsooth!

Yoo Hoo chaperoned, felt like a jerk,
As she marched them back to set it
    free.
Grumpy kids! Might as well add
    homework.
So she showed them the letter "C".

"C" is for cat", shc announced
As she carved it on their climbing
    tree.
But the kids watched the kitty who
    pounced,
And growled playfully, being free.

Yoo Hoo passed out new birch bark
    scraps
But she was mostly ignored.
And as hours began to elapse

Yoo Hoo became totally bored.

She left them with an assignment
And told them in no uncertain terms
"Get busy. Don't whine!" Then she
    went.
This would be their daycare mid-
    terms.

That's when Mama came for her
    baby
And Daycare scrambled up the tree.
These lions sport 10-inch fangs
    maybe,
But can't climb, zoologists agree.

She used those fangs on their birch
    bark
And everything that smelled
    mannish.
She chewed and growled until almost
    dark.
Then she snatched up her kitten and
    vanished.

Yoo Hoo met them coming back.
Excuse was, a big cat delayed it.
They had lost their homework,
    yackety-yak.
Teachers know this one: "The cat ate
    it".

Boys Do It Standing

It's a proud first time for young boys,
Peeing from a standing position.
Oh, the thrill of the splash and the
    noise!
I tell you, it feeds the ambition.

It's a glee that girls will never know
And opens the door to adventure.
There's an urge to put on a show.
That is one thing your Mom will
    censure.

As little boys grow they find time
To do it off of balconies.
And being math and science inclined
They see relevant analogies.

Probably this is the reason
Why boys are drawn to science and
    math.

Naughty little boys aren't just
    breezin',
They're establishing a career path.

Ben Franklin, as a bright young lad
Surely enjoyed such merriment
And probably this balcony fad
Led to an early experiment.

He let fly from up high in a storm
Hoping to prove electricity.
Luckily the test failed to perform
In spite of its simplicity.

But later when he could afford
A nice kite, he proved his theory.
We needed the guy. But oh, Lord!
As a boy he risked hara-kiri.

OVER THE EDGE

Humanity had a Golden Age.
Things were easy when the world
    was flat.
The rivers disposed of our sewage
Leaving us a clean habitat.

Rivers did stink when the water was
    low
But with the next flood it was
    cleared.
Everything went down the rivers
    though,
To the ocean where it disappeared.

The ocean current hauled it from
    there

And took it to earth's furthest rock
    ledge
Where, since it was heavier than air,
It simply spilled over the edge.

Gravity kept it close, I suppose.
It collects down under, somewhat.
But that odor that gets in your nose
Stayed down there, by the earth's
    butt.

It was a sustainable solution.
But Explorers popped that bubble.
Too bad. We never had much
    pollution,
And now we've got nothing but
    trouble.

PRIVATE PROPERTY

"You'll own nothing, and you'll be
  happy!"
Says the World Economic Forum.
"Work harder! Earn more!" said my
  Pappy
Like other Pappies before him.

Two visions. Two different futures.
So the tried-and-true is tied
With the new one, favored by
  moochers.
Let's ask a cave girl to decide.

She has things: A knife, three carved
  bowls,
Homemade outfits, sandals and
  more.

She scowled. I think she called us
  "buttholes".
Then she showed us what the knife
  was for.

The cave girl (let's call her Maria)
Defended her worldly possessions.
She had it right. Buenos Dias!
She didn't need any lessons.

Her things were a priority.
The cave girl thinks like us.
Which proves that we're the majority.
But we should fight like her. Not just
  cuss.

EATING INSECTS

I'm sure you've grinned through fake
    vampire fangs
Or a clean orange peel with no
    germs.
But imagine your kids and their
    whole gang,
Grinning through squirmy
    mealworms.

We might get there, but not yet.
I'm just playing with apparitions.
But we may have to eat bugs to get
Some control of greenhouse
    emissions.

They checked out 5 common insects

For emitting those gasses.
And you'd be shocked what all ejects
From those cute little crevasses.

But cows emit more just from eating
    hay,
When they belch and from you know
    where.
It's a lot, but how much does it
    weigh?
Nothing! It rises. It's just hot air.

It's music a farm boy enjoys.
Herds of cows aren't very quiet.
But until you can weigh that noise
We don't need an insect diet.

CHOOSE YOUR OWN

Ice Age tribes hanged their worst
    criminals.
In broad daylight. In public view.
No pious songs, no hymnals.
There were no jails. What else could
    they do?

There were protests at Council
    meetings.
Some wanted the practice revised.
They totally disrupted proceedings
To expound upon being civilized.

That was new. Those were big
    words.
But the Council was inclined to
    disagree.
What else could they do with guilty
    turds?

They deserved it, as anyone could
    see.

Non-lethal ideas were nixed.
In a roll call vote by voices.
The lethal part would stay fixed
But they agreed to offer choices.

All the gruesome choices listed
Would be carried out the same day.
Or, the condemned guy, unassisted
Could choose his own lethal way.

That's quite civilized for the times.
A year passed with no further
    outrage.
So how many died for their crimes?
Haha, nada. They all chose old age.

THE LETTER "D"

As we check in with Yoo Hoo's
    Daycare
Wolves have 'em up their tree and
    won't leave.
The kids are offering up a prayer,
Even before Adam and Eve.

So what might they ask of the Lord?
They want a pet. A wolf runt would
    do.
There was an odd-looking one they
    adored.
Was it even a wolf? No one knew.

The kids asked their babysitter,
"It doesn't look like a wolf, does it?"
Yoo Hoo had never seen such a
    critter.
But if it wasn't a wolf, what was it?

"D" is for dog", decided Yoo Hoo.
It was time for a new letter.
When she carved it, which was easy
    to do,
It seemed to fit even better.

Someone tossed jerky to the dog
Who vamoosed with wolves on his
    heels.
It sure looked like his epilog,
But he returned for more free meals.

Which begs the question, which is
    better?
Good dogs or a partial alphabet?
Dogs won. But don't laugh at her
    letters.
They would win out, but not quite
    yet.

A.I. Brain Transplants

Have you heard what Google is up
    to?
They're skipping ahead in evolution
With A. I. Transplants. A new you!
It's part of the Green Revolution.

They'll bypass current generations
Who would otherwise pollute,
And we'll get much less sinful
    nations
Which will please the Lord to boot!

Oops, I don't think Google gives a
    hoot
About the Evermore.
They just want your brain for a
    crapshoot.
That's what they'll use it for.

When your deal is completed
You get all human knowledge for
    free!
Of course, your old brain will be
    deleted,
And yearly updates will cost a fee.

You'll have to find a new job.
Also a new husband or wife.
The new you will be quite a snob.
You won't remember your old life.

For these little bumps in the road
Google Gemini is your escort.
She'll answer your questions in bar
    code
Through your personal USB port.

Someday when we all have those
Life shouldn't be so tense.
But you still might get punched in
    the nose
Because Gemini has no common
    sense.

Don't do this! It's a double-cross!
You'll be the smartest human, that's
    true,
But Google will always be your boss.
They get updates not for sale to you.

BATS

It's what cavemen got used to, I
    guess.
Sabretooths or dealing with rats.
But how could they clean up the
    mess
When they lived in those caves with
    the bats?

All caveman caves had prior owners
So the first caveman clans
Had to deal with vicious loners,
Like lions who had other plans.

Cavemen were good with spear and
    knife,
Although they got mauled, and some
    died.
But mostly the beast lost its life
And the men dragged the carcass
    outside.

Now it was *their* home! The clan
    cheered.
But they didn't eat the devilish cats.
So men went hunting and
    disappeared
Leaving ladies to deal with the bats.

Today this is called 'housecleaning'.
It's why mops were invented, no
    doubt.
Bat poo piles up, if you get my
    meaning.
They're like flies. You just can't keep
    them out.

Ladies swatted them with a thing-a-
    ma-jig.
Want to see one? It's a bit of a chore.
Just kneel in that poo and dig.
They got left on the old stone floor.

TYING THE KNOT

Cavemen were poor on their wedding
  day.
They had clubs and some rope. Not a
  lot.
The brides had sore heads, sad to
  say.
But it was legal when they tied the
  knot.

The groom knots the rope around her
  waist.
The bride yells but the priest will
  ignore it
And skip through the service in haste
In case the bride makes a run for it.

That's how it was in the Ice Age
When weddings were planned by the
  groom.
There was no such thing as being
  engaged,

Nor rings, you can safely assume.

Enough already? The girls thought
  so.
Boys wondered why they were upset.
But boys can be dense. Advances
  were slow.
Girls weren't equal just yet.

They are equal now, and then some.
Ladies will plan your wedding.
Most guys just smile and play dumb
But inside they're nervous and
  dreading.

Golden rings and a kiss seal the deal.
Girls of all ages adore it!
It's how they bring tough guys to
  heel.
But some grooms do make a run for
  it.

BUZZARDS

All birds were born of the sun,
Unlike the beasts and the fishes.
It seems risky, but this was done
According to the Great Spirit's
    wishes.

I don't know but I'm pretty sure
They lived in the outer reaches
So the light in their hearts is less
    pure.
At least, that's what history teaches.

They were sent down to earth and
    released,
Where social graces had fallen to
    naught.
They saw the gluttony of the beasts
Who pigged out and wasted a lot.

Carnivores ate just the "best parts".
Times were tough for a vegetarian.
Beasts killed mostly to be braggarts.
And no one cleaned up the carrion.

Not a bird in that pristine sky
Offered to help with the mess.
So the earth just stank. By and by
The worst piles began to incandesce.

Clearly something had to be done
And Great Spirit knew what to do.
He reached deeper into the sun
Where light was pure, and hearts
    were too.

He grabbed a vulture for this task
For this thankless cleanup deed.
All He had to do was ask.
The bird licked his beak and agreed.

"It's a rotten mess!" warned Great
    Spirit,
And He started to repeat it.
But the bird didn't want to hear it
"Lead the way", he grinned. "We'll
    eat it!"

THE LETTER "E"

Terror Birds were South American.
They were apex down there for Ages.
When the Isthmus traffic began
They rampaged north. It was
    outrageous.

What luck for those fowl carnivores!
Accompanied by nephews and nieces
They killed everything on all fours
And pecked them into bite-sized
    pieces.

Now they're gone, like many
    ancestors,
Because cavemen found a way to foil
    'em.
Since Terror birds were ground
    nesters
Cave kids swiped their eggs and
    boiled 'em.

It was common in Yoo Hoo's
    Daycare.
They had just boiled a "Terrible"
    egg.
Just a joke. It was sumptuous fare!

But the Mom went off like a powder
    keg.

So Daycare was (again) up the tree.
And the egg they were about to crack
Was the last there would ever be.
And the Terror Mom wanted it back!

So the kids did give it back.
Piece by piece they tossed her the
    shell.
But the egg they kept for a snack.
She didn't take it very well.

Her hubby, an old Terror Pop
Demanded she lay another!
But the old Mom decided to stop,
And she was the last Terror Mother.

"Let's say "E" is for this egg", said
    Yoo Hoo.
"Hard-boiled. I had almost forgotten.
Fried and scrambled are very good
    too.
You'll like 'em any way but rotten".

FUR LINING

Caveman Chiefs were not called
 Kings
Nor their wives called Queens, so
 we're told.
The Ice Age had no time for such
 things,
And metal crowns were cold.

It was tough just to stay warm
Which they did with creativity.
In the time before the next storm
There was a whirlwind of activity.

Men hunted, gals were innovative
To lessen whatever winter might
 bring:
Inventions we don't know the date of.
But a Chief found the coziest thing.

He killed a sabretooth, which was
 rare
And was skinning it back to the butt.
That gets left - no one wants dirty
 hair –

When he had a nice thought. Guess
 what?

He carefully skinned off that end
And made the hole big - he's so
 sweet -
Ending up with a cavegirl's best
 friend:
Cleaned up, it's a warm toilet seat!

Soon all the brides wanted these,
And of course the grooms want them
 to purr.
And they don't want their
 sweethearts to freeze,
But most of them got rabbit fur.

That's back when brides were bought
 and sold.
When Mom asked, "How much do
 you love her?"
Smart guys offered furs, not gold.
So Mom got a warm toilet seat cover.

MISINFORMATION

The Ice Age was a lot like today.
Their officials were misunderstood.
Like a tribal Chief, let's say,
Who did bad things, but his heart
    was good.

He worried he might lose his job.
So he reluctantly hired goons.
It made him sad, but there was a
    mob.
His dear sweet tribe acted like
    buffoons!

Men had brought news of Terror
    Birds.
He called it a rumor, nonsense.
He cursed them, but just for lack of
    words,
And his goons made some false
    arrests.

Their cave was turned into a jail.
Good folks were turned out in the
    cold.
The arrests had been on a large scale.
Every last man, all told.

It was the saddest day of his life.

The Chief said that, speaking to the
    ladies.
Then he barely dodged a thrown
    knife
And they told him to go to Hades.

The kindly Chief had them locked up
    too.
But that's what they had intended.
The cave was warm, but a cold wind
    blew
On the Chief and his goons, which
    was splendid.

Near the witching hour Terror Birds
    did come
And caught the Chief on his crapper.
They gobbled him with his bare buns
But spit out his warm fur wrapper.

They got the goons too, so the tale
    says.
So the Tribe awoke to jubilation.
There were no words this big in those
    days,
But he died of his own
    misinformation.

CELL PHONES

A day will come when everyone
Has a cell Phone of their own.
The phone company's work will be
    done.
All possible growth will be grown.

But no! This is free-market
    commerce,
Not state-owned or state-run.
They'll find new sales, for better or
    worse!
Capitalism is never done.

But where do they go from here?
Free market means they'll explore.
There's a universe of new markets,
    dear.
They'll do business in the Evermore!

Oh, not with Almighty God.
But what about His heavenly flock?
This is new so it may sound odd
But St. Peter just might like to talk.

Look at it like a phone company.
When we die they lose us to our fates.
For those with faults and we have
    many
St. Peter waits at the Pearly Gates.

He asks tough questions, the story
    goes.
He knows a lot but he's not all-
    knowing.
He's not the Almighty and it shows.
The line's slow, even for the
    churchgoing.

It would help if we could phone
    ahead
With our glowing list of highlights
To impress St. Peter *before* we're
    dead.
We'll be stuck with truth after last
    rites.

Phone companies will get Peter a
    phone
With the help of a good medium
So good deeds can already be known.
That would speed the line and help
    tedium.

Thus humans will invade the Holy
    venue
But we still might end up bereft.
Angels will devise a phone menu
That eats up all the time we have left.

THE TILT

The earth's tilt can be a bummer.
Although it does give us our seasons
Some whole Ages don't have
    summer.
But when we tilt I know the reason.

Good posture isn't always good.
Whenever the earth stands up
    straight
(Like a mother would say it should)
An Ice Age starts right on that date.

Great scholars have that much
    figured out.
But from there they use words like
    'depends'.
Don't be like that! For those in doubt
I'll explain why an Ice Age ends.

It plays out over thousands of years
Snow falls and big glaciers grow.
They're mostly in the North
    Hemisphere
And they move. So where do they go?

Of course the ice sheets creep south
As the North Pole is getting colder.
The glaciers are the teeth in her
    mouth
As the Queen of the north wind gets
    bolder.

In the regions of eternal snow
At the top of the world there is joy!
Now nothing can stop the ice flow
Toward warm lands which it will
    destroy.

If I were a betting man then
I would've bet on the ice.
There wasn't much room for
    cavemen
When the lands were squeezed in this
    vise.

As the glaciers reached their crest
And the North Hemisphere
    overloaded
The Queen sent a huge blast at the
    rest
And her catastrophe unfolded.

With that blast the tipping point gave
    way.
It tilted earth 2 degrees,
Right back where we should be – Oh,
    yay!
And the world began to unfreeze.

So you see? History isn't hard.
The reason science often fails
Is because scientists never guard
Against poo-pooing fairy tales.

TECTONIC PLATES

When we speak of Heaven's Gates
We naturally look to the sky.
But there are two possible fates.
We just might go to Hell when we
    die.

That's a horrible thought!
We've heard of the Fires of Hell.
Where the worst sinners go, and it's
    hot.
Right under our feet, so they tell.

That's where he lives, bad-boy
    Lucifer.
Put there by the **One Lord**, whom he
    hates.
But he stirred the earth from within
    her
And the crust broke into floating
    plates.

Mother Earth offers no excuse.

Doesn't even seem to care.
When her plates slip, and Hell breaks
    loose
It's the devil saying he's still there!

He could sneak out if he chose.
Could be lurking in your church
    steeple.
But he's content and his influence
    grows
Inside a lot of foolish people.

Is there no way to get rid of him?
Could we banish him from earth?
He's got his fire so hopes are dim.
But we have water. And we have
    mirth.

I'm just one guy, but I could pee
Straight down at him. Is that a sin?
I could douse his fire symbolically!
We all could! And just watch us grin.

YOO HOO CAN GRUNT

Ice Age kids were slow to learn
  letters,
But youngsters will figure it out.
Not so their elders and their betters,
So Daycare school itself was in
  doubt.

Irate parents showed up to watch
  class
On the day Yoo Hoo introduced "E",
And the Chief's wife expelled all her
  gas
When Yoo Hoo carved it on the tree.

The wife had colorful words to say
But there's no letters for their
  language
So it can't be written down anyway.
They mostly grunted in the Ice Age.

When she blustered about banning
  Daycare
(Which, by the way, was Yoo Hoo's
  word)
She said, "Duh", and a young lad
  declared,
"You left out the "A", you old turd!"

That was Bucky. She grabbed his
  britches
As Yoo Hoo's class climbed the tree.
And her eyes bugged like a witches'
When Bucky shed his pants and
  broke free.

But for all that, Daycare wasn't
  banned.
Her husband showed up to calm her
  struggles.
Last we saw, they walked off hand in
  hand.
She loved him. He called her
  "Snuggles".

But the Chief was a politician.
Didn't care what Yoo Hoo taught her
  runts.
Keeping the peace was his ambition.
So Yoo Hoo better work in some
  grunts.

And so, beside the letter "E"
She carved "G". The Chief was very
  blunt.
She gave in that much to Authority
And the kids learned that "G" was for
  "Grunt".

THE LAST NEANDERTHAL

He was the last of his kind.
A very hairy old feller.
A Neanderthal, totally blind
But a great storyteller.

There was nothing for him in Siberia
So they took him along by the hand
For good luck. That was the theory,
    ya.
And it worked. They came to a New
    Land!

Along the way Nerdy (his nickname)
Told tall tales from his youth,
But in Alaska he became
An oracle, with the ring of truth.

His mind came up to the present
And he felt a need to confess.
His tribe had been beaten. Not
    pleasant.
New tribes wiped them out, more or
    less.

The kids laughed. The new tribes
    were their kin!
So they asked about "where" and
    "how".
But his mind was way past what had
    been.
He was seeing the future now.

He pointed toward the new sunrise

And spoke of delicious
    "Mammoots".
But a cloud passed before his eyes
And he warned of new, dangerous
    brutes.

He said, "More will come, just like
    you.
Times will change. There'll be tribes
    galore.
Your tribe will be called the Sioux.
You'll be powerful in war".

"But not as strong as the white
    races".
And he waved toward the rising sun.
"They'll come. They'll have pale
    faces'
They'll get everything and you'll have
    none".

Well, that's a downer for the kids!
Quite a few were attending.
He meant their tribe would hit the
    skids.
They asked for a happier ending.

"It's true!" he said. "You'll be dirt-
    poor. Wow!"
But the blind man smiled then.
And spoke of Indian casinos and how
They would win it all back again.

QUEST FOR FIRE (AND PEACE)

Before cavemen could make fire
They found it. But suppose it went
    out?
They held a contest. You gotta
    admire.
That's what the human spirit is
    about.

It happened about every four years.
When young dudes tended the fire.
And wouldn't you know? They were
    volunteers!
"There will be a Quest!" blared the
    town crier.

They were the heroes, or would be,
Of an Ice Age Olympic race.
The Chief picked the best four,
    basically.
And gave them last rites, just in case.

It was August, with no time to lose.
They spread out, trying to beat their
    friends.
Of three there was no further news.
We assume they met horrible ends.

But one young warrior returned,
With hot coals to save his destined
    tribe.
Soon a bonfire roared. How it
    burned!

So much joy, it was hard to describe.

That tribe would become the Sioux
    Nation
And win a great victory – a coup!
Well, some say great, some say
    damnation.
It depends what tribe you're talking
    to.

Their fight with Custer's cavalry
    corps
Went Hollywood now - just acting, of
    course.
And if they gave out Oscars for that
    war
Custer might beat out Crazy Horse.

I don't know if they fought hand-to-
    hand.
They should have. All leaders should.
Then our armies could disband,
Which would promote the general
    good.

Sitting Bull and President Grant,
The big Policy Makers,
Should've fought a duel. Don't say
    they can't!
The only losers would be
    undertakers.

THE CHOCOLATE

Since Great Spirit made the universe
His troubles have seemed to
  increase.
Mankind came next, which made
  things worse,
So He made chocolate to keep the
  peace.

It just has that virtue about it:
It makes everyone feel good.
So chocolate clouds such as space
  would permit
Searched for grumps to cheer up if
  they could.

Earth was in its dinosaur days
When a cloud rained chips and bars.
They loved it. It became a craze
And dinos grew fatter than boxcars.

Chocolate weather was all the rage
Beasts slurped it like a barnyard pig.
The last cloud came during the Ice
  Age
Which is why those beasts got so big.

It was gone before Adam and Eve
When the devil showed up with his
  apple.
If Eve had chocolate I believe
She'd have scorned him and built a
  chapel.

With no chocolate clouds anymore
It took a toll on the human spirit.
That's why we got Dark Ages and
  war.
But there's hope now, as I hear it!

They found chocolate trees in the
  Amazon.
Hurrah! That's what we've been
  needin'.
It's our best chance to bring world
  peace on
Since the Garden of Eden.

World peace is *so* close, dude!
And our foreign aid setup *so* handy.
But we send cash and ordinary food
When we should send chocolate
  candy!

THE LETTER "F"

What kept the Cavemen alive?
If you say "brains" I won't call you a
   liar.
But what else was needed to survive?
If you had been there you would say
   fire.

So fire gets taught, as a rule
Where there is no written speech
And in Miss Yoo Hoo's Daycare
   school
It was a popular thing to teach.

Please don't be judgmental of Yoo
   Hoo.
All kids play with fire and get burned.
All kids need an Ouchy or two
To remind them of what they
   learned.

Yoo Hoo made a fire, doing it right.
You could say she made a fire from
   scratch.
Her tribe used flint and pyrite
Long before they invented the match.

The kids divided the firewood pile
And as the daylight was dwindling,
Every child ended up with a smile
When they sparked up a fire in their
   kindling.

None too soon! Mortal danger did
   loom.
At that moment, as darkness fell,
Dire Wolf eyes appeared in the
   gloom.
And the pack was hungry as well.

It was a fine, teachable moment.
The snapping beasts feared the
   blaze.
But it was just a postponement.
Wolves are smart. They'll wait for
   days.

As the fires died to embers
And the lead wolf stood up to blitz
Yoo Hoo counted her D̲aycare
   members
And passed out some leather mitts.

She bounced an ember off the lead
   wolf's nose,
And laughed and called him a mutt.
And when he yelped and turned he
   exposed
His rump; so he got one in the butt.

In just moments the wolves learned
There is something even more dire
Than themselves. And dang it, it
   burned!
And the kids shouted, "F" is for fire"!

THE HAPPY SNOWFLAKE.

The first snowflake of the Ice Age
Fluttered down of her own free will.
Pure, translucent, under-age,
Nature's baby. We'll call her "Jill".

She was covered by millions of others
Over centuries, but have no fear
Snowflakes are airy. No one
    smothers.
And we'll keep track of her here.

Ice Ages go on forever.
Ask cavemen who couldn't outlive
    them.
They did amazing things, but never
Had patience like snowflakes.
    Forgive them.

Then earth warmed. Was Jill still
    there? Maybe.
They all melted, the snowflake
    daughters.
Last was Jill, the first snowflake
    baby.
Still Jill, but now a drop of water.

Exhilaration! Her first in a while

As down a rivulet she flowed.
She tried and found she could smile!
The first time since she snowed.

A stream! A river! Then a dull lake.
That wasn't fun. No it weren't.
But there was a city water intake,
And she felt the tug of that current.

It was such a rollercoaster ride!
She wished she knew who to thank.
But the turbulence finally died
In a suburban toilet tank.

Footsteps. What was this now. A
    human?
From scuttlebutt that was the best
    guess.
There was a splash and sudden
    boomin'.
And Jill was flushed into the mess.

Jill's still there in the filthy wastage
Dodging toilet paper and crap.
But she can't start a new Ice Age
So long as she's in that toilet trap.

PLEASE AND THANK YOU

I would touch up human decorum
If I was assigned by the Almighty.
I might sponsor a public forum
On being more polite, alrighty?

What I want is more "please" and "thank you' s
Going forward. We can't change the past.
And violence dominates the news.
I watch and walk away aghast.

Maybe rudeness ruled the Ice Age too.
They had their share of jackasses.
But with no written record to view
The cave people all get passes.

Our earliest written records
Hint at greed and warlike ways,
And massacres and bloodthirsty Lords.
Not much civility in those days.

We've been like that ever since.
That's why the news is what it is.
The lack of politeness makes me wince.
But now I can fix all this!

If I may stretch my assignment a bit
I will *make* people be more polite.
And if they don't obey, I admit,
I will…what's that word?…oh yeah, I'll *smite!*

That's when the Almighty will fire me
For taking the do-gooder thing too far.
Well, He's smarter than I'll ever be.
I'm no Almighty. I don't belong thar.